*"Do you wan...
asked*

Ever the hero, Samantha thought and realized, she'd never had a hero in her bed before. Never a protector. Never someone who actually cared a whit about what she was feeling. Yet her wanting him was tinged with fear since she didn't quite know how she would react to his touch. Whether the vampire within would rise up, out of control as passion also grew.

Already she could feel the heat of the beast inside her, warming her skin. Loving the taste of him in ways that were not necessarily good. But she didn't want it to end. Maybe that was selfish of her, but she wanted to know what it was like to be loved with gentleness and caring.

"No. I don't want to stop."

Dear Reader,

October is a funny month in New York City. Sometimes it rains, sometimes it snows, sometimes it's sunny. And in the stores, there's the anticipation of Halloween with candy and costumes. Although children don't usually trick-or-treat in my building, I still buy candy and wear a witch's hat just in case. Maybe this year, a group of goblins and vampires will show up so that I won't have to eat a whole bag of chocolate myself. Speaking of vampires, October is a banner month for our readers. We've got enough paranormal and adventure so that you'll want to keep a light on at all times.

New York Times bestselling author Sharon Sala returns to the line with *Rider on Fire* (#1387), which features a biker chick heroine who is led on a mystical journey to her long-lost father. Of course, she finds true love on her quest…and danger. RITA® Award-winning author Catherine Mann continues her popular WINGMEN WARRIORS miniseries with *The Captive's Return* (#1388), where an airman finds his long-lost wife. As they race to escape a crime lord, will they reclaim their passion for each other?

You'll love Ingrid Weaver's *Romancing the Renegade* (#1389), the next book in her PAYBACK miniseries. Here, a sweet bookworm is swept off her feet by a dashing FBI agent, who enlists her aid in the recovery of lost treasure. Make sure to wear your garlic necklace with Caridad Piñeiro's *Temptation Calls* (#1390), in which a beautiful vampire falls for a mortal man. And while she's only known men as abusive, will this dashing detective tempt her out of the darkness? This story is part of Caridad's miniseries THE CALLING.

Have a joyous October and be sure to return next month to Silhouette Intimate Moments, where your thirst for suspense and romance is sure to be satisfied. Happy reading!

Sincerely,

Patience Smith
Associate Senior Editor

Please address questions and book requests to:
Silhouette Reader Service
U.S.: 3010 Walden Ave., P.O. Box 1325, Buffalo, NY 14269
Canadian: P.O. Box 609, Fort Erie, Ont. L2A 5X3

TEMPTATION CALLS

CARIDAD PIÑEIRO

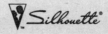

INTIMATE MOMENTS™

Published by Silhouette Books

America's Publisher of Contemporary Romance

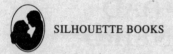 **SILHOUETTE BOOKS**

ISBN 0-373-27460-2

TEMPTATION CALLS

Visit Silhouette Books at www.eHarlequin.com

Printed in U.S.A.

Books by Caridad Piñeiro

Silhouette Intimate Moments

Darkness Calls #1283
Danger Calls #1371
Temptation Calls #1390

*The Calling

CARIDAD PIÑEIRO

was born in Havana, Cuba, and settled in the New York metropolitan area. She attended Villanova University on a presidential scholarship and graduated magna cum laude in 1980. Caridad earned her Juris Doctor from St. John's University, and in 1994 she became the first female and Latino partner of Abelman, Frayne & Schwab.

Caridad is a multipublished author whose love of the written word developed when her fifth grade teacher assigned a project—to write a book that would be placed in a class lending library. She has been hooked on writing ever since.

When not writing, Caridad teaches workshops on various topics related to writing and heads a writing group. Caridad has appeared on Fox Television's *Good Day New York,* New Jersey News' *Jersey's Talking* with Lee Leonard and WGN-TV's *Adelante Chicago,* as well as being one of the Latino authors featured at the first Spanish Pavilion at the 2000 Chicago BookExpo America. Articles featuring Caridad's works have appeared in the *New York Daily News,* Newark, New Jersey's *Star Ledger,* South Florida's *Sun Sentinel, latinolink.com, Variety Yahoo! Online News* and *Waterbury Republican-American.*

Caridad has been married for over twenty years, and is the mother of a teenage girl.

To my husband, Bob Scordato, who puts up
with my insanity, makes sure we all aren't wearing pink
underwear and has always believed in me! Thank you
for your never-ending love and support, Bubba.

Chapter 1

Spanish Harlem, 2004

As lives went, both of hers had sucked. Still, life went on and on and on, and everyday things had to be dealt with.

Samantha Turner bore the weight of the heavy grocery bags without complaint. They were for her shelter, The Artemis Shelter, a halfway house where women and their children could heal and find a way out of the abusive relationships in their lives. With her help, many families had already broken the cycle of violence that had cursed Samantha's long existence. She was finally doing something positive with this life.

A clerk from the local Gristedes supermarket would have delivered the groceries, but after being trapped indoors all day, Samantha wanted to breathe the night air. To savor the activity of the city that never slept. To revel in the city's humanity so she could prepare for another day of battling its cruelty.

She rounded the corner onto her street and noticed a few youths from the neighborhood and two younger children lingering on the stoop next to the shelter. It was nearly midnight. Too late for them and their hip-hop music blaring from the boom box on the railing.

Despite the distance and the dark, Samantha identified Juan Williams, his little brother and sister, plus an assortment of kids from Juan's self-made posse. Mrs. Williams worked the late shift at a nearby hospital and Juan was supposed to take care of things when she was gone.

He did anything but.

Samantha quickened her pace. She could get the younger Williams children inside and in bed where their mother expected them to be. It was the kind of thing they all did in the neighborhood, watching out for each other.

In the years since Samantha had brought the Artemis Shelter to this part of New York, life had gotten better for this block and that sense of community had slowly spread to the adjacent streets. Funny that her little point of light came from something darker than most could begin to imagine.

Samantha was halfway down the street when a car came sharply around the corner. Tires squealed as the car swerved, but the noise was not enough to hide the sound of a weapon being locked and loaded. Voices urged on the shooter as he stuck himself out the open window.

So many in harm's way. Too many.

Knowing even as she did so that it would raise questions she didn't want to answer, Samantha dropped the bags and accelerated beyond human speed. She grabbed the two youngest children and carried them down the stairs to the shelter's lower floor. She shoved them into a far corner before returning to street level to help the others.

The loud *pop-pop-pop* of gunfire erupted in the night. Bullets flew, striking sparks where they hit brick and stone, splattering blood and more where they connected with flesh and bone. The teenagers scurried to get away, their bodies jerking and thrashing as they failed to avoid the line of fire.

As Samantha grabbed one youth, a bullet tore into her upper back and another hit lower, in her side. She kept moving, carrying the teenager to the stairwell while the shooter continued to fire.

Then as suddenly as it began, it stopped. The car peeled away with another angry squeal of its tires and loud rejoicing from its occupants. Anger rose up sharply within her. The animal she'd been for too long wanted vengeance. But the human side of her knew that instead of going for their throats she should memorize the faces of those responsible and note the car's license plate number.

Besides, Samantha couldn't chase the car. Others needed her. Even this far down the block, the smell of gunsmoke and blood was strong. *Too strong.* Samantha battled the urge threatening to overwhelm her.

She took a deep breath. In the distance, a siren was fast approaching. It grated on her sensitive hearing and she reached up to cover her ears.

A familiar hand touched her shoulder.

"The children can't see you like that," he said, motioning with his free hand to her face. "And you're hurt."

"I'll be okay, Ricardo, but… Is there anything you can do for the others?" Samantha gestured to the bodies littering the stoop and sidewalk.

Ricardo slipped off his jacket and draped it around her

shoulders, revealing his naked chest and a low-slung pair of pajama bottoms. He'd clearly run out of his small *botanica* on the corner of her block without bothering to change.

"I'm not sure—"

"Someone has to see to them and you're right. I can't go back now," Samantha said. She couldn't afford to have her secret revealed to anyone else. It was bad enough that Ricardo had discovered the truth about what she was so soon after she'd moved to the neighborhood. Right now, there were too many things tempting the animal to emerge—her anger, the smell of the blood and the pain from her injuries.

Ricardo handed her the keys to his place. "Go and rest. I'll do what I can."

After quickly giving Ricardo a description of the occupants and the car, she fled to the safety of the *botanica*. Once inside, the smells of herbs, flowers and candles calmed her heightened senses. She moved slowly toward the back of the shop and to Ricardo's living area.

She'd been there often. Many in the neighborhood suspected them of being lovers. None could have guessed the true nature of their relationship.

Samantha slipped off his jacket and draped it over a small sofa then she walked to his bathroom to wash the blood off her hands. How many had been killed? She should've saved more of them. Guilt flooded her.

But gazing up at the mirror, she saw nothing. No guilt. No anguish. No image. She hadn't seen her reflection in the one hundred and forty-one years since she'd become a vampire.

She ran her hand over the burning spot high on her shoulder. There was but a half-closed hole beneath her fingers as her body slowly expelled the bullet that had ripped into her flesh.

Farther down, along her side, at the ragged exit wound

where the bullet had passed completely through her, the bleeding had stopped. The wound was already beginning to knit.

It would take a little longer, but not much. The healing would leave her weak, but even as a human she'd been accustomed to pain. No matter how much she despised the truth, neither of her lives had been free from violence.

Samantha headed for Ricardo's rocker. It reminded her of her mother and how she'd swayed Samantha to sleep as a child. She curled up on the rocker's worn wooden seat. "*Maman,* will it never end?"

New Orleans, 1860

Please let it end. Let it end soon, Samantha thought as she huddled protectively around her swollen belly, trying to shield her baby.

But the blows didn't stop. Not for a long time.

He used his fists against her face. He kicked at her, the sharp toe of his polished black boot like a knifepoint as it connected with her arms and back and even with her belly when he found an opening around the defenses she erected in vain.

Samantha didn't scream. The screams would only make the beating worse. Maybe even hurt others.

Last time she'd screamed, one of the field hands had rushed in to help her. Her husband had beat the man to within an inch of his life and the field hand hadn't lifted a hand to protect himself. A black man wouldn't dare harm his white master.

Nor could a Creole woman like Samantha. Many would consider her lucky to have landed a husband like Elias Turner, a handsome and charming sharecropper.

Samantha herself had thought so when Elias had wooed her at the tavern where she worked. It had once been owned by

Samantha's parents, before her father's weakness for drink had ruined the business and her mother had worked herself to death. As an orphaned servant girl of mixed blood in a city where blood still mattered, Samantha couldn't have done better than the attractive and prosperous Elias Turner.

What she hadn't realized was that his captivating smile and charisma hid hands that too easily became fists. Or that Elias would much rather win some quick cash at cards than labor out in his fields. And worse yet, that Elias hated that she was the descendent of slaves, a mixed-blood.

Samantha had tried to make a good home for Elias, hoping that he would change. She prayed her actions would mellow the violence he too often unleashed against her and his slaves. With her careful attentions, their small home gleamed and she always had an appetizing meal waiting for him. In bed there was nothing she wouldn't do or allow done to keep Elias's mood good, even though at times what he asked made her feel lower than the cheapest whore in the French Quarter.

When she'd caught him looking at her swollen belly just a few weeks ago, she thought she'd finally seen something there—the start of the change she'd been working so hard to achieve.

She'd been wrong. Oh so wrong.

Elias hated that the child she bore wouldn't be pure. As he beat her, he spat out his disgust for her and the baby she carried. Accused her of tricking him with her beauty and making him forget she wasn't much better than his ebony-skinned slaves. When he was finally done venting his anger, he stormed from their home without even a glance back.

Even though he had left, Samantha continued to huddle tightly on the floor, bloodied and in pain. She prayed and fought not to scream as one spasm and then another tore through her. She didn't want Elias to come back and hit her again because of the noise. She didn't want anyone else to come in and risk a beating.

With each spasm of pain, Samantha bit down hard on her lower lip, tasting coppery blood and the salt of her tears. Something warm trickled down the side of her face from her brow. Between her legs, she was damp with whatever was escaping her body. It pooled beneath her, wet and sticky.

Samantha beseeched the God who so far hadn't heard the cries of the women in her line. She pleaded and begged that the child within her would not know this same despair.

Morning fled and afternoon came. She lay there, unable to move. The puddle beneath her was cold now, as was she. She was weak and almost delirious from the agony racking her body.

It was dark when one of the field hands finally found her. As his gentle hands cradled her close, she finally let herself rest.

Cool bathed her forehead. It coursed down her face and along her neck, rousing her. She remembered only vague bits and pieces of the last few hours.

Slowly she opened her eyes and gazed into an undeniably masculine face. His eyes were dark, nearly black, and intense, but somehow comforting. She recognized the face, but it took her a moment to remember—Dr. Ryder Latimer from the plantation down the road.

"How do you feel?" he asked, his tone filled with concern.

Samantha tried to sit up, but pain lanced through her side and lower. She gasped and reached to rub a comforting hand over her belly, only…

"My baby. Is it…?"

"I'm sorry," he said and abruptly rose from beside her bed. He strode over to the small cradle at one side of the room and tenderly picked up a tiny quiet bundle. Dr. Latimer gently placed his burden in her hands. "I thought…" He paused, battling with his own emotions before continuing. "I thought you'd want to see her before… This is your daughter."

Tears slipped down her cheeks, stinging against the cuts and scrapes left by her husband's hands. She let the tears come. *Her daughter.*

With hands that trembled, she cradled the child to her and lifted away the bit of blanket that covered her baby's face. So small. So perfect, Samantha thought. She had the shape of her grandmother's face and maybe her brow. A small thatch of jet-black hair like Samantha's own. Pale white skin, nearly colorless in death.

In death.

"Why?" Samantha asked, although she knew why. Her daughter was dead because Samantha was too weak to protect her.

"I can call the sheriff. He can—"

"Arrest my husband for beating me?" They both knew nothing would be done.

Dr. Latimer sat down on the edge of the bed. His gaze was somber, but full of anger. "You don't have to stay here. I have plenty of work at my place."

"He'd just follow me. Cause problems for you. Even worse, he'd hurt the people here. Better that he hurt only me." But it hadn't been only her. She cradled her daughter's immobile body tight to her breasts. They tingled and, in response, milk began to flow. There would be no mouth to suckle them.

The doctor stood, looking down at her, hesitant. Clearly uneasy. There was more he had to say. Samantha knew it wasn't good news.

"Tell me. Whatever it is, just tell me now."

"The birth and the beating. It tore you up badly inside. I'm not sure you can carry another child."

Samantha closed her eyes at his words. Her daughter dead and any hope for another gone with her. "Maybe that's for the best. It'll keep another child from knowing pain."

He said nothing, just walked to the door of her bedroom. "When you're ready, there's a pretty spot over at my place. Beneath a cherry tree and overlooking the river. You're welcome to it for the child."

She was touched by his kindness and all that he'd done. "Thank you, Dr. Latimer. If there's ever anything I can do for you…"

He hesitated at the door, clearly considering her words. Finally he said, "You can live, Mrs. Turner. Just live."

And then he walked out, leaving her alone to grieve.

A tear slipped down her cheek, as cold as her memories.

So much killing. So much pain. More than her rightful share in her long and seemingly interminable lifetimes.

Swaying back and forth in the rocker, battered both mentally and physically, Samantha withdrew into herself. Arms wrapped tight around her chest, teeth worrying her lower lip.

Samantha didn't know how much time had passed when she finally sensed Ricardo's presence in the room. "You were somewhere else, *amiga*. I didn't want to disturb you."

She stopped her rocking and gave him a tired smile. "Thank you. Are they gone yet?"

He shook his head. "It'll be a few more hours before the police go, but they'll be back in the morning to ask more questions."

That was the last thing she needed—questions that might reveal her secret.

"The groceries are in the kitchen. I put the milk and other

things in the refrigerator. I told the lead detective that I was just returning from shopping, but given my current state," he motioned to his attire, "I'm certain he didn't buy my story."

The story wouldn't hold up anyway, Samantha thought. A visit to the local market would reveal who had made the purchases. "Thanks for trying." She laid a reassuring hand on his thigh. Beneath her fingers she sensed his blood, pulsing with life, and she shivered in response to her preternatural desire.

"Are you cold?" Noticing her deep chill, he said, "You need to feed."

Samantha confirmed his observation and Ricardo left the room, returning moments later with a blood bag for her. "Sara just brought this today. I figured the freshest would be best."

She thanked him before bringing the bag to her mouth.

Already partially in her vamp state because of her actions when saving the children and the wounds she'd suffered, the prospect of a fresh feeding completely transformed her. Her fangs erupted, elongating. Saliva dampened her mouth in anticipation. She placed pressure on the skin of the bag until her fangs punctured the thick plastic. Greedily she sucked down the blood. Energy coursed through her veins, bringing with it warmth and renewed strength. Some blood spilled onto her lips, spicing her mouth with its unique flavor.

Stingy that even one drop should escape her, she licked her lips. She laid her head back against the rocker and took a deep breath, then another. Calm slowly settled within her, replacing her earlier anger and sadness. Her fangs retracted and all other traces of her vampire nature receded. With renewed energy, she could exert control once more.

Meeting Ricardo's gaze, she smiled. "I'll return to the shelter once the police have gone."

"Stay until morning and I'll walk you back."

It was an old argument. Whenever she returned from patrolling the neighborhood, she'd go by the *botanica* to sit, talk and feed if need be. When it was time to go, invariably Ricardo would suggest she stay.

She examined his face in the dim light cast by the lamp on his nightstand. There was no denying he was a handsome man. Hair the color of fertile earth hung to his shoulders in silky waves. Luxuriant green eyes reminded her of the deepest part of a pine forest. Tonight his gaze was tender and filled with concern for her.

But Samantha had no interest in any man. Not even one as incredibly desirable as Ricardo. Men had only brought pain into her life.

"You know there can never be anything between us," she finally said.

Ricardo reached out to caress her cheek, but she reared away out of habit. She didn't like being touched.

His full lips thinned to a tight line. "I would never hurt you. I'm not like whoever did this to you."

No, he wasn't, she thought. From the moment he'd sensed what she was with his unusual healing powers, he'd been a source of support. But his understanding wasn't enough to overcome her many years of suffering. She didn't trust men. Wasn't sure that she ever would. But worse yet, she didn't trust herself or the violence buried within her. The demon inside her was always just beneath the surface, waiting to emerge.

She laid a hand on his thigh once more. "I know you wouldn't cause me pain. It goes against everything you are. But I can't make the same promise."

"*Querida,* you could never—"

"Hurt someone?" she said. She touched her chest. "Inside me there's violence. I battle it every second of every day. I wanted to kill those boys tonight—the ones who shot Juan and his friends."

He didn't say anything, apparently sensing it would only lead to an argument. "I will set my alarm so you can go before sunrise."

Samantha shook her head. "There's no need. I can feel the dawn coming. I'll know when to leave."

Ricardo nodded. He slipped beneath the covers of his bed. *"Buenas noches."* He shut off the light.

"Good night." She huddled in the rocker again. In the quiet, she heard the susurrus of his breath, deepening as sleep claimed him. The beat of his heart slowed and blood pumped sluggishly through his veins. The smell of him was sumptuous with the life she lacked.

She was still weak from her earlier wounds and the heat of her transformation came upon her quickly, with her awareness of him as prey. Her fangs emerged. Her eyes adapted to the night, allowing her to see every inch of him: the pulse point throbbing along his neck as his head lay against his pillow, the fine network of veins just below his skin.

With her acute senses, the enticing masculine scent of his sweat was strong. The warmth of his skin as alive as if it was pressed to hers. It would be easy to break through that thin layer. Much easier than through the plastic blood bag. And his blood—it would be so hot and fresh on her lips, fill her with an energy the bagged blood couldn't match.

Samantha hugged herself tight and buried her head against her knees, battling her urges. She had to go. Her control was too weak from all that had happened.

There was still activity outside, but it had lessened considerably.

She concentrated on those outdoor sounds: the shuffle of

feet against the sidewalk; the slam of car doors; the rasp of equipment going back into storage areas; the murmur of voices.

Human voices in the night, unsuspecting of what was near.

The sounds became her sole focus, keeping the demon inside her contained until finally, there was silence.

Taking a last look at Ricardo as he slept, she hurried down to the kitchen where she gathered her things and left.

Dawn would not have come soon enough to spare her friend.

Chapter 2

NYPD Detective Peter Daly never made it home after the drive-by shooting. From the moment the call had come in, just past midnight, he'd been on the job.

It was just as well. He didn't really have any reason to go home.

The sights at the morgue that morning had been grim. Three dead, all below the age of sixteen. Another one in critical condition. Amazingly, three had survived with barely a scratch.

He was still puzzling about those three as he stood on the sidewalk, examining the scene of the shooting once again. The Crime Scene Unit was supposedly finished here, but Peter thought there had to be something they'd missed. Something that would explain how three kids had escaped a fusillade of bullets.

He stepped backward, off the curb and into the middle of

the street where the car had paused. With as many rounds as the Tec-9 could fire, you didn't need good aim. Just point and shoot. That was enough to hit almost anything within close range.

Which didn't explain how three of the children had somehow gotten away. Nor could the children explain it either. All they recalled was that they were suddenly whisked into the stairwell next door. The hangers-on in the neighborhood, religious semisuperstitious types from what Peter could see, had murmured that an *angelita* had saved the children. It was a miracle.

Peter didn't believe in miracles or maybe even Heaven for that matter. But Hell. Hell was right here, he thought as he ambled back to the sidewalk, searching for any clues the Crime Scene Unit might have missed. Along the street and stoop there was nothing. Down in the stairwell of the building next door, he hit pay dirt.

Some drops of blood. Just a few on the top step leading down to the shelter's lower level. Along the railing, what appeared to be a smear of blood. Removing a kit from his jacket pocket, he swabbed at the drops and the smear, and then safely tucked the evidence away for analysis.

Glancing up at the shelter, he wondered if anyone there had seen anything. Or if someone within had been responsible for the supposed miracle. And the blood.

As Peter turned, he caught sight of the garbage cans. A veritable source of information. He popped open the lid on the first receptacle. Nothing but recyclables. Lifting the lid on the next one, he noted the refuse from last night's dinner. Taking off his jacket, he undid the cuff on his white shirt and rolled it up. Then he gingerly placed his hand in the garbage—a job he totally hated—and rooted around. Barely below the surface he came across something tucked into a bag from the local grocery.

The *santero* down the block had claimed to have been shopping. Peter grabbed the bag from the garbage. He undid the tied handles to reveal a woman's blouse. Easing the blouse out using the plastic of the bag, to avoid contaminating the evidence, he noted the bloodstains and two glaring bullet holes—one high up on the shoulder, the other along the rib area.

Curiouser and curiouser. Peter slipped the blouse back into the bag and returned to his car. He stuffed the blouse into an evidence bag and noted the details about his discovery. Placing the blouse and the swabs in his trunk, he decided to visit the local market to see just who had been shopping last night.

As Peter walked to the Gristedes, just a few blocks away, he was struck by the neat and tidy conditions of this area. There was a sense of safety and community he hadn't expected in this neighborhood. But then it hadn't been the least bit safe for those involved in last night's shooting.

At the market, Peter had no luck with the clerks or manager on duty. The night shift had just left. But the manager offered to let Peter view a tape from the night before.

There was a clear shot of a woman making a purchase shortly before midnight. A beautiful woman wearing a shirt much like the one Peter had discovered in the garbage.

"Do you know who she is?" Peter asked, motioning to the image paused on the screen. Had she been another victim? If she'd been hurt, why hadn't she shown up in a local hospital?

The manager shrugged. "I've never seen her before. Maybe one of the clerks has."

One by one the clerks were called into the manager's office and one by one they all failed to recognize the woman in the video. Peter thanked them and added the tape to the other evidence in his car.

Then, figuring he had nothing to lose by following his instincts, he walked up the short set of steps to the door of the Artemis Shelter, identified by a small bronze plaque. Vaguely he recollected that Artemis was a warrior goddess in Greek mythology and wondered who had chosen the name for the shelter and why.

A young black woman with a toddler balanced on one hip answered his knock. "May I help you?" Hostility came off of her in waves.

Peter held up his shield for the young woman to see. "NYPD. I'm here investigating last night's shooting. Do you mind if I come in?"

"Do you have a warrant?" she asked, maintaining her position smack in the middle of the doorway to bar his entry.

"I just want to ask a few questions. Find out if anyone saw anything last night."

"Come back when you've got a warrant." She was about to slam the door in his face when he reached out and grabbed the edge of it.

"There's no need for this. Just a few questions." Although given all that he'd found between the garbage can and the grocery store, he'd have enough probable cause for a warrant.

When the door fully opened again, the woman from the grocery store stood behind the young black woman. He'd thought her beautiful in the grainy video. Up close, she was stunning.

Jet-black hair fell in thick waves, framing a heart-shaped face with just the hint of a cleft in her chin. Her skin was the palest of café con leche and her eyes were large and a startling shade of crystalline blue. Barely thirty years of age.

Peter felt poleaxed as she focused her cool gaze on him. "I'm sorry," she said. "Sofia is just a little protective. What can we help you with?"

Her tones were cultured, with a bit of an accent. Southern, not that he was any kind of expert.

"Detective?"

Embarrassed at his almost juvenile silence, Peter stammered as he said, "I'm investigating last night's shooting. I'd like to speak with you, if you have a moment."

"Actually, breakfast is a rather busy time—"

His interest was replaced by irritation. "Miss—"

"Ms. Turner," she corrected with an almost regal lift of her head.

"Ms. Turner. We can either do this here or down at the precinct, which would take substantially more time out of your busy day." He took out his notepad from his jacket pocket to stress his point.

The young black woman protested at the same time as the vision of beauty said, "Detective, I'd rather not—"

"Ma'am. Please understand. Between the videotapes from the grocery and your garbage can, I have probable cause. I'd rather not complicate this with a warrant."

What little color she had fled from her face and for a moment he worried she might faint. Instead, Ms. Turner stiffened her spine. "Sofia. Could you make sure the children are ready for school while the detective and I share a word in the kitchen?"

Sofia nodded curtly and glared at him as she stepped away.

Ms. Turner opened the door wider, giving him space to pass, and held her hand out in invitation. "Please come in."

Peter stepped inside to a whirlwind of activity. Ms. Turner hadn't been kidding when she said it was a busy time. Sofia and another woman were handing out lunch bags and checking schoolbooks for at least half a dozen children of varying ages and ethnicities.

Ms. Turner walked down the hall adjacent to the parlor and past stairs leading to the upper floors of the converted brownstone. At the far end of the hall, Ms. Turner took the stairs leading downward and he followed.

On the lower level was a large dining room that opened onto a small, neatly kept courtyard. The tiny patch of grass was a bright green from the spring rains and someone had been busy planting flowers.

The dining room table was still littered with the remains of breakfast. At least Ms. Turner was being truthful about that.

She walked to the kitchen located at the front of the building. There was a door at one end and he suspected it was the one that opened into the stairwell where the children had taken refuge last night. "May I?" he asked and at her nod, he confirmed his suspicions.

When he closed the door, Ms. Turner motioned to the worktable. "May I get you something? Coffee? Beignets? I just made them fresh this morning."

"Ben-what?" he asked, confused, but he took a seat at the table. He hadn't eaten since an early dinner the night before.

"French donuts." Ms. Turner poured a cup of coffee and placed it in front of him. The aroma was wonderful. Beside the cup, she added a pitcher of steamed milk and a small silver dish with brown sugar.

"Donuts, huh?" He added sugar and milk to the coffee, took a sip and nearly groaned at how tasty it was.

Ms. Turner didn't wait for his answer. She gave a wry smile as she placed a plate of the ben-donuts before him. "They say the way to a cop's heart—"

"Is with donuts? I don't think so," he teased back. Then he picked up one of the square bits of dough, which were still warm, and took a bite. This time he did groan, "Or maybe it is. Thank you. I haven't eaten in a while."

Samantha examined the detective, trying to make some sense of him. He was in his early thirties, but there was a weariness in his stance and gaze that spoke of having seen too much of life. Handsome, if you liked those Nordic types. Thick hair streaked with varying shades of blond fell in uneven layers around his face. The raggedness of the haircut was boyishly appealing in an "I don't care" kind of way. He had pale hazel eyes tinged with the tiniest bit of light green.

As they'd walked through the shelter, she'd noticed he was tall and physically robust, inches over her five foot seven height. A rangy kind of build, though with more strength and bulk than a runner. Possibly kept there by the way he ate, she thought with some humor as he devoured the plate of beignets.

"Would you like some more, Detective?"

A wash of pink colored his cheeks and he wiped his mouth with a napkin to remove all traces of powdered sugar. "No, thank you. Do you mind if—"

"We get to the questioning. I'm not sure I can be of much help." She hoped to avoid any questions that would involve her in the investigation. She couldn't afford anyone delving into her background too deeply. Plus, despite a feeding earlier that morning, she was feeling weak once again. Losing control in front of this detective…she didn't want to think about it.

"A tape from the store shows you buying groceries just before midnight. Since I walked the route, I'm guessing you got back to the block as the car drove by."

"I was already in the shelter when I heard the gunfire."

"Really?" He raised one sun-lightened eyebrow. "I found a blouse in the garbage. Just like the one you were wearing at the grocery store."

"Coincidence? Passersby regularly use those garbage cans."

"Passersby with two bullets in them?"

Samantha smiled and held her hands up to emphasize her point. "Do I look like I've been shot, Detective?"

He eyed her up and down and then asked the unexpected. "Mind if I check?"

Peter watched as his request registered. Her blue eyes grew hard like diamonds. Her jaw worked up and down a few times before she croaked, "Excuse me?"

"You posed a rather interesting question, Ms. Turner. Did you expect me not to take you up on it?"

Her eyes blazed with anger. "You, sir, are no gentleman."

Definitely not a New Yorker. Problem was, everything about her made him think of sultry Southern nights and sex, which were the last things he should be thinking about. Recovering, he said, "You can ask one of the other women to come down and act as a witness. Or we can go—"

"Down to the precinct," she finished for him even as she reached for the buttons on her blouse.

"Please turn around, and lower the shirt."

She did as he asked, revealing the upper part of her back, unmarred except for a myriad of faint uneven lines. Old scars?

She gazed at him over her shoulder and he felt as if he'd been kicked in the gut. There was so much pain, so much fear and anguish in her gaze she couldn't hide it.

Without thinking, Peter laid a finger on one of the pale lines. Her skin was as cold as ice.

She wrenched away from him. "Don't." She grasped the opening of her blouse as she whirled to face him.

Peter took a step back, shocked at his own actions. At what he was feeling about this woman he'd only just met. He'd had enough of women in his life, after all. "I'm sorry. I didn't—"

"Do you need anything else, Detective…? Come to think of it, just what is your name?"

"Daly. Peter Daly from the twenty-third. Who did that to you? Mr. Turner?" Instinctively his hands curled into fists as he imagined exacting punishment on her behalf.

Anger emanated from him. Samantha cringed and stepped away. "It was a long time ago and I'm over it." Not that she really was. Her reaction to his touch had proven that. "Please. Just go."

He hesitated, clearly troubled, but then he reached into his pocket, withdrew one of his business cards. "If you need anything, just let me know."

Samantha didn't know how to read his offer. Had she just gone from suspect to victim? If the former, he'd be back.

As for the latter, the good detective was obviously a man used to not only dealing with violence, but meting it out when necessary. And more violence was the last thing she needed in her life. "Goodbye, Detective."

"Not goodbye, Ms. Turner. We'll be seeing each other again."

Any other woman might have viewed a further visit from the handsome detective with anticipation.

It was an indication of the state of her undead life that she viewed it with dread.

Chapter 3

Samantha Turner was a frickin' saint. Or at least, that's what most people believed along the block where the shelter was located. The funny thing was, when asked if they'd had any personal contact with Ms. Turner, most said they'd never seen her. The remainder had only seen her once or twice.

The one thing they all agreed on was that the area had gotten better in the three years since Samantha had opened the shelter.

A one-woman frickin' social improvement campaign.

Peter didn't know why he was so annoyed about the supposed sainthood of Samantha Turner. Maybe it was because he knew that behind a woman's beautiful face and virtuous ways was often a soul filled with deception.

His ex-wife had been beautiful. She'd been sweet and oh-so-needy of Peter's attentions. Warm, willing and waiting for him, even when he'd worked the long hours required of a beat cop. He'd been working his way up the ranks so he could provide for a wife and family. Oh, how he'd looked forward to the day when they could have children and buy that home they'd always wanted.

Peter slapped shut the file on his desk. Glancing into the squad room, he realized no one had even noticed. There was too much going on.

Just as there had been too much going on in his life for him to notice what his wife was doing when he was gone. Eventually she had walked out on him with her lover and their life savings.

Beautiful is as beautiful does.

Samantha Turner was an exceptionally beautiful woman.

How had she come to be where she was? Who had marked her back with those scars?

Criminal any way you thought about it. Which meant there had to be a record of it somewhere. With that information, he might get a more complete picture of the enigmatic head of the Artemis Shelter. Maybe that would help him deal with her, know how to get her to open up and provide whatever information she had about the shooting.

More than anything, Peter wanted to nail those responsible for the killings, but he needed more evidence. So far, he'd been unable to track down the car. The license plate number had revealed that it had been reported stolen a few days earlier. It might not ever be found if it had been turned over to a chop shop. And the descriptions provided by the sole witness weren't very specific—described a large number of youths in Spanish Harlem.

So, Ms. Turner might be the key to breaking this case and because of that, he needed to know more about her. He went through the various databases available to him, from the local ones to those kept by the Feds. Hours passed. His investigations yielded nothing except a Social Security number and minimal financial information. For anything more detailed, he'd have to ask for help. Escalate the investigation. If she'd been a suspect, he wouldn't hesitate to bring in others and expose her private life to greater scrutiny. But Samantha Turner wasn't a suspect. She'd done nothing wrong. There was no reason to sic anyone else on her…yet.

He had a job to do and if he stepped on some toes while doing it, so be it. At least that's how he felt until he remembered the faint lines on her back and the look she'd given him.

He recognized that almost haunted expression. He'd seen it in the mirror more than once in the months after his wife's desertion.

So, this time, he would cut Ms. Turner some slack. Respect the pain he'd seen in her eyes. Leave it and her alone.

That's what Peter told himself as he put his fingers back on the keyboard. That's what he told himself as he listened to the M.E.'s phone call about the evidence he'd turned in the day before. The blood couldn't be typed nor could any DNA samples be extracted. Had Peter bagged the evidence properly? Had the materials been close to any chemicals or excessive heat that might have compromised them?

With a tired sigh, Peter answered the M.E. and hung up.

Glancing at his watch, he realized that with little happening in the investigation, he might as well call it a night. Head home to the fourth floor walk-up apartment in downtown Manhattan that wasn't the house in the suburbs with the neatly manicured lawn he'd always wanted. That thought made him remember the tidily kept courtyard at the Artemis Shelter. Was Samantha the one who'd been busy planting flowers?

She shouldn't be on his mind. She was just a witness. Not

a suspect. Not a victim. At least not on his watch. Whoever had failed her had to deal with that guilt. Not him.

He had enough to handle. He didn't need any woman in his life, especially one with as many secrets as Samantha Turner.

Which was why he called himself a fool when he drove away from the precinct and headed uptown to ask Ms. Turner a few more questions.

Chapter 4

Samantha was in bed when the call came from her longtime vampire friend, Diego. His youngest charge was missing.

Samantha was weak. Weaker than she should be after multiple feedings, but she couldn't refuse her friend's plea for help. Even if it meant going to the downtown vampire club she detested.

The Blood Bank was an odd kind of place, hidden in a dark alleyway and unknown to humans—except those who had a desire to experiment with dark elements. Those people managed, by word of mouth, to spread the news about the club's existence. As for the demons, they, too, let others know—this was where the normal rules of the human world didn't apply.

The Blood Bank provided demons with a place to let loose and to feed from the fine stock of blood acquired from a select group of blood banks and butchers. Even, occasionally, from a willing human participant, although the club had strict rules about siring humans on the premises.

The humans, on the other hand, went to the club for many reasons. The naive ones believed the fake vampires put on a good show. Others wanted to believe the vampires were more than actors and got a kick out of possibly mingling with the undead. And finally, there were those true believers who were always ready to search out a chance to embrace the darkness.

A darkness in which she had lived for too long, when what she desired most, like Diego's poor lost little vampire, was the light. Only all that was light and good was far beyond her reach, Samantha thought, and then for some reason, the good-looking blond detective came to mind. He was as forbidden to her as the light: first for being a human; second for being a man.

As Samantha, Diego and his lover, Esperanza, strolled into the club, the crowd parted before them, as if sensing their in-human power. All of the booths and tables near the back of the club were filled, but that didn't deter Diego.

He examined all the spaces and then walked to a booth populated by a group of Goth-looking kids barely out of their teens. He met the gaze of each of them and in a soft voice, which did nothing to diminish the menace behind his words, said, "You were just leaving, weren't you?"

Two of the three abruptly rose, but one young man lingered, despite the exhortations of his companions that it was time to go. He stared at Diego insolently, the sneer on his face accented by piercings on his upper and lower lips. As he smiled, the sharp points of fangs became visible.

A wannabe, she thought, failing to sense that otherworldly energy that set apart her kind from the many humans within the club.

"Actually, I'd planned to stay a little longer," the young man said.

Samantha laid a hand on Diego's arm when he moved toward the Goth. "Please. He's just young and foolish—"

Diego cut her off abruptly, his normally light blue eyes beginning to glow with the unnatural light of his transformation. "Then he will learn a painful lesson."

In a blur of movement, Diego sat beside the young man, holding his hand in a viselike grip. Fear appeared in the young man's eyes as he stared at Diego's face. Although Diego had yet to morph to his full vamp state, he showed a tiny bit of fang in a display of power.

It worked.

"Please, man. I'm going. I'm gone."

When Diego released him, the young man scurried away to meet his friends, who had melted into the packed club.

Diego smiled and assumed his human face then motioned for her and Esperanza to join him in the booth.

With a huff, Esperanza said, "I hate this place, Diego."

Diego stroked her long auburn hair tenderly. "I know, *querida*. But this is where Meghan is most likely to show up."

His missing charge, Meghan, being the reason all of them were sitting in a place they generally despised. For vamps like Samantha, Diego and Esperanza, the Blood Bank was a last resort when they needed a real feeding, one not from bags or beef blood. Here, they could occasionally find a human willing to provide them with a quick sip.

Nearly a century earlier, in a club much like this in San Francisco, Samantha had first met Diego and Esperanza. She'd been looking for a vampire she'd suspected of abusing one of the girls in the shelter where she was working as a cook. She'd wanted to make sure he wouldn't trouble the young woman again, but the vampire had been killed earlier that night in a fight with Diego.

She'd been fearful of Diego's strength until she'd realized that, like her, he believed in using his power to make things right.

Which was the reason they were all here tonight, Samantha reminded herself as she tried to find the young vampire in the crowd.

Meghan was only twenty-one years old. Forever twenty-one. When they'd first met her two years ago, Meghan had only been a vampire for a few months, which meant she couldn't tolerate the effects of daylight and missed feedings.

In the vampire world, only the strong survived and strength came with age. If weak vampires survived the usual challenges like sunlight and garlic, they had to keep out of the way of stronger vamps who could, if they wanted, put a quick end to their lives for the slightest of infractions. Crosses and stakes were low on the list of dangers because people just weren't scared anymore thanks to the proliferation of the undead in the media.

But Meghan, the missing vampire, was pathetically weak. So much so that Diego had taken pity on her when she'd attempted to kill her sire, thinking that would free her vampiric curse. Diego had given her a place to live and offered his human servant as company when Meghan wanted to stay awake during the day like a human. Like Samantha, staying indoors to avoid the strong noon light and slipping outside for a chance at normalcy when the sun was weak.

Meghan had run out on Diego's servant a few days earlier, and she'd been missing since. This club was the one place Meghan was likely to return to, either to feed or go after her sire once more.

Samantha carefully scoped out the crowd, but there were

a number of coeds who matched Meghan's description—long blond hair, slender, petite and young.

A waitress came by, dressed in a getup that Marilyn Manson would envy—a tight black merry widow and black lace stockings. "May I get you something?"

"A round of blood. Nothing but human," Diego said with a dismissive wave of his hand.

The waitress rushed to comply, returning to the bar that was kept stocked by payments to health inspectors who turned a blind eye to the unusual libations the club offered.

Samantha glanced back at her two friends as they waited for the server to return.

Diego was as stunning as always, in a charcoal-gray silk Helmut Lang suit and black silk shirt that exposed the pale white skin of his chest. His nutmeg-brown hair was down to his shoulders and straight. His eyes were a marvelous blue— clear and bright like an ice-fed mountain stream. He turned heads, but not just because of his looks. There was something almost regal in his carriage. Probably because before he'd been turned, Diego had been a Spanish lord. A betrayal during the Spanish Inquisition had resulted in his imprisonment and torture. It was deep in the belly of a Spanish prison that he'd been "converted"—although not in the way the priests would have imagined.

As beautiful as Diego was, Esperanza was as plain, but with a good, if sometimes selfish, heart. The one thing Esperanza hated was sharing Diego's attention with the women he'd saved over the years.

Women like the missing Meghan. Women like Samantha.

Strays and lost souls who often frequented places such as the one they were now visiting.

But unlike other clubs with an obvious theme, the Blood

Bank had none. Only walls, ceilings and a bar painted black. The booths, chairs and tables—where they weren't scarred and exposing whatever material was beneath—were, of course, black.

It matched the hair and clothes of most of the people in the place. Or at least, most of the wannabes. Meghan's blond looks would have stood out, except that occasionally, like tonight, the bar got its share of first-timers who were there to check out the wild stories they'd heard. Unfortunately, most of those club virgins had a tendency to look like Meghan.

"So, do you think she'll show up tonight?"

"Who knows?" Esperanza replied with an impatient shrug.

The waitress delivered their drinks and hot on her heels was none other than Blake, Meghan's sire, looking as surly and punk as ever. As the waitress departed, Blake planted his fists on their table. "Wannabes."

Wannabe *humans* he should have said, since all of them knew what the young vampire thought of them. Samantha didn't know anything about Blake's background, but if he'd suffered even a small bit of the violence that she and her friends had endured during their human lives, he would better understand why they chose not to harm others now that they were virtually immortal.

"That outfit looks like something out of the seventies," Esperanza taunted, motioning with her head to Blake's chain-studded black jeans and jacket

"Well, I think I look right fine." His words had a hint of a cockney twang to them, an affectation he'd adopted when someone told him he looked a bit like Billy Idol. Samantha almost laughed out loud as he followed his words with an obviously practiced sneer.

Instead, she said, "Meghan is missing again, Blake. Have you seen her?"

"Been there, done that." He studied her face. "Are you okay, because you look a bit wan." Then he quickly added, with a wiggle of a pierced brow, "Could help you out, love, if you know what I mean."

Impatiently Diego said, "Just tell us about Meghan."

"Little chit was here last night on one of her rampages." There was a bit of swagger in his stance as he continued, "Think we finally settled things between us. She didn't seem to mind putting the bite on me in the alley."

Vampire-to-vampire feeding being the ultimate of pleasures, Samantha thought. Esperanza had the palest touch of embarrassed color on her face while Diego's showed nothing but annoyance at Blake's locker room talk. Much like humans, polite vampires didn't discuss intimate details. Feeding on another vampire was as intimate as having sex—dangerous, mind-blowing, near-death sex.

"That was a risky thing, *amigo*. With Meghan in one of her states, she could have easily ripped your throat out," Diego said.

Blake leaned forward until he was almost in Diego's face. "Jealous, old man?"

In a flash, Diego wrapped his hand tight around Blake's throat and squeezed hard. Blake fought to free himself, but Diego's grip was too strong. When he finally released the punk vamp, he said, "Respect your elders, Blake. As for Meghan, she is under my protection. And so I ask, do you know where she went?"

Blake took a step back from the table, rubbing his throat. "I think she wanted a snack after our little get-together. She left with some old dude late last night and didn't come back."

"Thank you," Diego said and dismissed the young vamp with a nod.

Blake hurried off, melding into the crowd on the dance floor as best he could with his shock of pale hair.

"You don't think she drained the human?" Samantha asked.

"I saw nothing in the news about it." Diego gave her a long look. "Blake was right when he said you look a little…fragile."

She shrugged off his concern. "Three children died last night."

"I heard." There was understanding in his voice as he added, "And you feel responsible?"

"Wouldn't you?" After being turned, Diego had seen the change as a way to atone for his earlier selfishness. As his strength had grown, he'd taken in those who were weaker, protecting them when necessary.

"You were hurt, *mi amiga.*" He covered her hand as it rested on the tabletop, but he didn't give her a chance to answer. "*Sí,* you're very weak. Your skin is chilled. You should have said something."

Samantha pulled her hand away and hid it beneath the table.

Diego shot her a hard look then tossed down the shot of blood, grimacing afterward.

When Esperanza went to pick up her drink, he stayed her hand. "It's stale. Let's find ourselves a snack and after…" He paused and glanced at Samantha, "You can restore yourself from one of us."

"Diego—"

"*Querida,* do not argue. You are more frail than I have ever seen you. I imagine you slept the whole day. I know how much you must hate that."

She couldn't argue. Lassitude had chased her for the better part of the day, preventing her from assisting the women at the shelter. Instead of a vamp schedule of daytime slumber and nighttime activities, she'd always tried to mimic a more human life. It was necessary if she wanted to run the shelter and help others avoid the violence that had doomed her to her vampire state.

Without answering, she watched Diego and Esperanza go in search of sustenance.

Samantha perused the inhabitants of the club, hoping to spot Meghan, but if the confused young vampire was here, she wasn't making herself known.

But the others in the building… That was a different story. Samantha could smell them. Their sweat, filled with lust and longing. She felt the warmth of the human bodies pressing close. Their life forces spilled through the place, and mixed within them was the more powerful energy coming from those who coveted that life force.

As weak as she was, Samantha could still feel the auras of the other vampires. Blake. Diego and Esperanza. At least two others working their way through the crowd. She transformed slowly so she could better perceive the other vampires, and as she did so, the crowd parted and Diego approached.

The blood-fueled energy coming off him rolled over her like a tsunami. He'd had his snack and his veins rippled with life. When he stood and held out his hand, his force was almost a physical presence, urging her to rise no matter how much she detested needing what he would give her.

She placed her hand in his. His skin was warm. Pink tinged his normally pale cheeks.

"Are you ready, *mi amiga?*"

She wasn't sure she was. It had been quite a long time since she'd fed off a human, but she remembered the power in that kiss. The energy and passion fused to create a state that approached Nirvana. The thrill in subduing someone weaker and taking what they might not want to give. It was that last violent aspect that made her shun feeding on humans, even those who appeared to be willing. Once the first pain occurred, they were never willing.

As for feeding on another vampire… It would be a first for her. She'd never been weak enough to require that kind of sustenance. She hoped it would be the last time. Unlike other vampires who took great pleasure in such activities, Samantha had no interest in continuing with the practice.

Sensing her hesitation, Diego applied gentle pressure to her hand. "Let's go somewhere more private."

At his urging, they walked to the back of the club to a series of small rooms. Billed as private dining rooms, Samantha could only imagine what was happening within. Vampires feeding on vampires and humans alike. Humans sharing a tryst as they gave in to their darker side.

An unfamiliar vampire appeared before them, blocking their way. He held out his hand and Diego slipped him some money.

The vampire pulled aside a curtain and led them down a dark hallway. He unlocked one room and disappeared.

Diego held open the door for her. "Are you ready?"

Chapter 5

The room was not much bigger than a closet. A small uncomfortable-looking bed spanned one wall and along the other was an assortment of chains, straps and bindings.

"You don't expect that you and I—"

"No, Samantha. I know what your life has been like. I would never ask you to exchange your virtue for what I offer." He cupped her cheek, his touch that of a friend and not a lover.

"And you offer—"

"A way for you to quickly rebuild your strength. Otherwise, it may take days and many more feedings before you are right. With Meghan missing, we all need your strength."

Samantha couldn't imagine feeling as badly as she had today for several more days. Nor requiring that many more feedings. Her blood supply was hard to come by, and with as many people as there were in the shelter, she risked discovery by feeding too often. "Why are you offering this?"

"I was a selfish and foolish young man. It's why I am the way I am. But now I wish to help. In exchange, I only want the friendship you have offered for all these years."

His words brought tears to her eyes. He was one of the few men in her life who'd ever shown her any kindness. He and Ricardo… And the good detective.

Diego brushed away a tear. "I believe you would be more comfortable if we did this standing up, *no?* Minus the accoutrements, of course."

"Of course," she said, watching as he slipped off his jacket and his shirt, revealing his chest and neck to her.

Each muscle on his body was delineated beautifully, as if a sculptor had chiseled the fine lines into the palest of marbles. He was almost too beautiful to be real, and she reached out, laying her hand on his chest just to remind herself that he was.

His skin was still warm from his feeding, but nowhere near a human temperature. Nevertheless, the heat of it blazed against her skin, chilled as she was from the injuries to her system.

Diego bent his head, exposing his neck.

A spark of warmth came to life inside her. She could feel her fangs elongating, slipping downward past the edge of her lower lip. His heartbeat, slow and steady, called to her.

Rising on tiptoe, feeling a bit woozy from the transformation that had drained the last of her strength, she inhaled the scent of him, savored it before she grazed his neck with her fangs. A shudder worked through his body and he grew hard against her.

"Diego, don't." Her voice sounded way too feeble to her own ears.

"I cannot help it, *mi amor. Por favor,* just feed. Before I forget that I am an honorable man."

Samantha met his gaze and realized the truth of his words. There was only so much he could bear. And she had no choice any longer. A damp sweat had erupted on her chilled skin as her body began to fail.

With a small prayer that they both knew what they were doing, Samantha bit down on his neck and fed.

The rush that had come from feeding on Diego was indescribable. From the first taste of his blood, energy had surged through her, charging every atom in her body with incredible potential. Invigorating all her senses until everything seemed more alive than ever.

She'd taken only a few sips, afraid of the intensity of that kiss. Afraid of the passion that might rise within her. Sexual urges that would need to be assuaged had she fed even a drop more.

She avoided passion. In her life, passion had invariably led to pain. First her husband. Then the vampire who'd turned her. It was why she avoided any kind of involvement.

Once passion entered the mix, everything was sure to change.

Even a hint of desire was enough to incite her fear, which was why she didn't linger with Diego. When she reached the shelter just past midnight some of the effects of her feeding had worn off, but not entirely. Like someone who was over-caffeinated, she was unable to rest. Unable to remain confined. So she slipped into the night, leaping from rooftop to rooftop as she surveyed her neighborhood to make sure all was right. It was something she regularly did to keep the neighborhood safe. Even though she rarely saw anyone during her solitary patrols, she knew her neighbors believed her responsible for the improvements in their lives.

She paused her patrol after an hour to watch the fast rush

of clouds across the face of the moon. A storm was on its way, she could smell it. When the first drops arrived, she turned her face to the sky and let the chill rain wash over her. It cleansed away the smell of Diego and his blood, cooled the heat of her skin from her transformation and the feeding.

The calm lasted only until she returned to the shelter. A flat of bright salmon-colored impatiens and a note from Sofia waited for her on the kitchen table. *Detective Daly dropped by with these flowers and some questions.*

She didn't know what to think about the flowers. She took them out to the small brick patio just beyond the French doors to catch the spring rain.

The flowers sat there for the rest of the night and into the early morning while she worked off some of the blood-induced energy by making lunches for the children and working mothers and preparing that morning's breakfast.

Dawn was just breaking when Sofia came down, rubbing her eyes and yawning. "You're up earlier than usual."

"I couldn't sleep."

"Thinking about the good detective?" Sofia asked as she made a pot of coffee.

Yes, Samantha thought, but she shook her head. "Nope. Just worried about a friend." Which wasn't far from the truth. The night had come and gone with them finding out nothing about Meghan's whereabouts. It wasn't like they could go to the authorities for help.

As she'd put the impatiens on the patio, she'd let herself imagine how the good detective might react if she asked for his assistance.

Hello, my friend Meghan is missing.

Any distinguishing characteristics?

Why, yes. Fangs and a bad temper when deprived of blood.

He would think she was certifiable. Not that she cared what he thought.

Then she had little time to think about anything as the morning rush commenced, with the women and kids shuttling in and out of the kitchen, preparing for another day.

He was a stupid fool.

Why had he expected her to be home last night? She was a beautiful woman. She wouldn't sit around the shelter day in and day out. His cop's intuition told him there was something about Samantha Turner that was far from saintlike.

He'd felt like a total idiot as he'd thrust the flat of impatiens into the hands of the young black woman who'd answered the door earlier in the day. Her sullen mood had dissipated to some extent, but it hadn't kept her from issuing a warning. "Ms. Turner has no interest in men."

With those words, she'd slammed the door in his face and left him pondering all night long the meaning behind them.

Given the nature of the shelter, and the scars he'd seen on her back, it seemed likely that Ms. Turner's aversion to men had to do with a relationship with one man that had soured her on the species in general.

And you're about to remedy that? The annoying little voice in his head had challenged him for the entire drive back to the shelter this morning.

He really had no more information than he'd had the day before. Which meant that unless she abruptly changed her tune about her whereabouts on the night of the shooting, it would do little good to see her again.

So instead of walking up her stoop he headed to the end of the block, to the store where his one supposed witness lived and worked.

Peter gazed through the large display window at the various items for sale along with the *santero's* services. Rumor claimed he was a healer, although Peter was reluctant to put much faith in gossip. Doctors healed. This guy was probably a con man robbing people of what little they had left from their social security and welfare checks.

Not that Peter could do anything about it, even if that was the case.

As he walked to the door, the sign that said Closed flipped to Open.

Inside, it was not what Peter had expected.

In the anteroom of the shop, one wall held an assortment of candles and books related to various religions. A glass-topped display counter ran along the opposite wall and bore an antique cash register. Within the counter, religious medals and pins made of gold, silver and semiprecious stones gleamed. Behind the register stood the healer himself and beyond him, bookshelves filled with dried flowers and herbs alongside sacred statues and other items of devotion.

"May I help you, Detective Daly?" Ricardo asked.

"Mr. Fernandez," Peter said with a nod of his head. "I wanted to confirm the information you provided the other night."

Peter walked into the back room of the shop. Here at the farthest wall, there was a small altar holding a large statue of a saint, although he couldn't identify which one despite his earlier life as an altar boy. Assorted candles were scattered along the altar, together with an assortment of small bowls and dishes that held an eclectic mix of items—flowers, tobacco and some coins.

Peter motioned to the altar. "This is—"

"To Catholics, Santa Barbara. But to those of us who prac-

tice *santeria,* it is Chango, one of the strongest of the deities."
Ricardo followed Peter then sat in one of the chairs in the
back room.

Peter turned to look at him, waving his hand at the woven
grass mat on the floor and the chairs circling the area. "What
exactly do you do back here?"

"Worship. The Supreme Court says it's allowed, you
know." As he spoke, Ricardo crossed his arms in a casual
stance, but there was some anger in his words.

Peter sat in one of the chairs opposite Ricardo. "Do you
do your 'healing' here?" he asked, trying to keep his voice
neutral, but knowing he failed miserably.

Surprisingly, the other man took Peter's contempt in stride.
"I'm not asking that you believe, Detective. But I know I've
helped others with my abilities."

Peter flipped through his notes before asking, "You say you
helped one of the teenagers that night."

Ricardo nodded. "One of them was still alive when I got
there, but bleeding badly."

"Was it a mystical help or—"

"Plain old medical help. I applied pressure to his wound
and tried to do what I could. I was a medic in the army before opening my store." Peter suspected there was more to that
story than he was letting on, not that it mattered to this case.

"And how about Ms. Turner? How did you help her that
night?"

"Detective. I've already told you. I was the only one on the
street that night with the children."

"Right. So tell me how it is that Ms. Turner was the one
who purchased the groceries at the store? Groceries in your
possession immediately after the shooting."

There was no trace of emotion on the *santero's* face. Not

even a flinch or a narrowing of the eyes. "I went to the shelter. Ms. Turner was already inside when I took the groceries from her."

"In your pajamas? And you walked right into the line of fire?"

"I'm a healer, Detective. What did you expect?"

He'd expected the *santero* to do exactly what he was doing, Peter thought. Cover up for Samantha Turner. Peter had no doubt she'd been there that night. Maybe even had a hand in saving the lives of the children who'd survived. But if she had done so, she had to have been injured. The blouse and the blood in the stairwell gave mute testimony to that fact.

"Did you heal Ms. Turner after she was shot that night?"

Shaking his head, Ricardo rose from his chair and motioned for Peter to leave. "I think we've exhausted this line of questioning, Detective."

Peter followed Ricardo back to the counter. "Did you heal her? Off the record."

Ricardo narrowed his eyes as he considered him. "Off the record?"

Peter nodded.

"What Samantha has, I can't heal."

Something akin to dread filled Peter's gut. "She's sick? Is it—"

"It's not a sickness like you can imagine, Detective. It's in here," Ricardo said and motioned to a spot above his heart.

"I know she's had it rough. I saw the lines on her back."

Ricardo seemed almost physically jolted by that revelation. "She doesn't show them to many people. She must trust you."

He didn't want to contradict the other man by telling him that he'd given Samantha no choice. Not that they were what he'd expected. But having seen them, he'd recognized that she'd entrusted him with something very personal and very painful.

Peter said nothing else, just closed his notepad and headed for the door.

"Detective."

Peter stopped and turned.

"Don't make her sorry that she trusted you."

Chapter 6

The morning sun was still weak and she was still in over-drive from Diego's blood. Not to mention that a flat of salmon-colored impatiens called to her to be planted.

Samantha let Sofia know where she would be, grabbed a large floppy-brimmed hat and walked into the yard. The buildings nestled close together kept the yard in partial shade for most of the morning. It wasn't until noon that the sun was high enough to bathe the yard with light.

Perfect timing actually. At her age she could tolerate weak morning sunlight, but not anything stronger. At least, not for long. She hoped wherever Meghan was, she had taken shelter. As young as she was, she could die quickly from overexposure.

She picked up the flat of impatiens and began on the left side of the yard. The sun would bathe that area first as it trav-elled to the west. The border along this side already held a col-lection of vegetable plants. The small garden cut food costs and there was nothing like the taste of a ripe tomato picked off the vine.

Small shovel in her gloved hand, floppy hat securely on her head, she worked quickly, transplanting the impatiens from their small plastic containers to the rich earth. As she worked she occasionally glanced up at the sky, keeping a careful watch for the sun.

She had bordered the vegetables when she heard the slide of the French doors. Sofia stood in the courtyard, Detective Daly beside her.

Merde.

"You have a guest." Sofia didn't wait for Samantha's reply. She left the detective to find his own way.

Samantha wasn't about to encourage him to stay. As he walked toward her, she picked up the flat and walked to the back of the yard to continue with her gardening. She dug a few holes and was reaching for a container when he stood beside her.

"I'm sorry to bother you again."

She refused to look up. Instead, she slipped a plant in each hole and tamped down the soil around the roots. "I've already told you I know nothing about what happened that night."

He crouched down to her level. "I got a call a short while ago. We found the car and CSU is already working it."

She finally faced him. A big mistake. Unlike the other day when he'd been looking a little haggard from lack of sleep, he had a fresh-faced glow on his tanned face. His hair—that shaggy streaked blond hair—hung along the edges of his face, itching to be brushed aside. She fought her awareness by saying, "And that's supposed to mean?"

"We may get some prints or other evidence. But that's still not as good as an eyewitness."

She rose and shifted to work on another section of the border.

He followed, but didn't crouch down beside her again. Instead, he pitched his plea while standing, his hands tucked into the pockets of his serviceable dark gray suit. He jangled his change as he spoke. "Your friend Ricardo wasn't at the scene. That's obvious from talking to him."

She shrugged and continued digging. "Ricardo says he saw the car and the shooter."

"*I* never said there was only *one* shooter."

Peter watched as his words made her pause. She fumbled with the shovel before resuming her methodical planting. "Ricardo mentioned it to me."

She was lying. He didn't need to see her face to know it. He could tell from the tension in her body. The muscles in her shoulders had tightened beneath the pale blue long-sleeved T-shirt she wore with faded jeans that hugged every curve.

"A defense attorney will shred Ricardo's testimony. That may create enough reasonable doubt for those killers to walk."

She finally turned her gaze on him. Her earlier flush had faded. Now she looked rather pale. "I didn't see what happened."

"They'll kill again, you know. They're like animals. Once they get a taste of fresh blood, the urge doesn't go away."

His comment made her blanch even more and sway. He reached out to steady her, but she wrenched away. "Don't touch me."

Peter gritted his teeth and took a breath. "I'm sorry. Again."

She glanced down at her hands before looking up at him and then beyond. He followed her gaze, but could see nothing since the sun was coming up over the roof of the building next door. Samantha tucked the last small pack of flowers beneath one of the low-lying bushes then hurried to the house.

Peter followed her, intent on pleading his case, hoping she would admit the truth.

Once inside, she tossed her hat and gloves on a small table then poured herself a cup of coffee. She didn't offer him one.

Which disappointed him. First, because the lady made a mean cup of coffee. Second, because he knew she was blowing him off. He wasn't about to let her get away with that. "May I have some?"

A small smile quirked her mouth. "Presumptuous aren't you?"

He shrugged. "I've been called worse."

That dragged a chuckle from her. "I imagine you have, Detective."

"Peter. You can call me Peter. Remember?" he said as he sat at the kitchen table.

Samantha eyed him intently, trying to get a read on the detective. Was the investigation making him linger, or was it something else? Despite her age, or maybe because of it, her womanly intuition was rusty. She intentionally hadn't dealt with the man-woman game since escaping the vampire who sired her. That had been nearly one hundred and forty years ago.

"Detective," she said now. "Have you had breakfast yet?"

"There's no need, ma'am. Unless you have more of those square donut things."

He dragged a smile to her lips again with his honesty and with his boyish grin at the mention of the beignets. Turning from him, she poured him a cup of coffee and microwaved a small pot of milk to warm it. When she placed both before him on the table, she finally answered him, "No beignets today, Detective."

"Peter."

"Just some buttermilk biscuits."

"Homemade?" he asked with hopefulness.

She crossed her arms and smiled. "Are there any other kind?"

"Would you join me if I had one, or maybe two?"

She'd told herself not to encourage him to stay and yet here she was doing just that. And even considering his offer to join him, not that she had need of any food. While she might enjoy the tastes of what she prepared, only blood provided sustenance. Until the sun had entered the courtyard, Diego's blood had energized her, but now that strength was beginning to fade. Once Sofia left for class and the good detective departed, she'd have to grab a snack from the small refrigerator in her room.

"I'm not really hungry, but I'll keep you company. It's the least I can do to thank you for the lovely flowers."

"No, it was the least *I* could do to apologize for yesterday. For touching you. I shouldn't—"

Samantha gave an angry slash with her hand to silence him and looked away. "That's okay. I'd rather not discuss that."

She almost jerked back when he cupped her chin and urged her to look at him. "I'm sorry. And you're cold. Are you okay? You're pale."

She hated the concerned look on his face. "I think it's time you left, Detective."

He didn't correct his name again, as if aware that it would do little good. Biscuits and coffee forgotten, he rose, and she walked him to the front door.

"Not all men hurt, you know."

Samantha gripped the edge of the door, battling for control as anger rose in her. "And you know this because you're an expert in what men do?"

All boyishness fled from his face. He motioned to everything around them. "I see it every day, Samantha. I know what *some* men do. But I know there are other men who want to make things right."

Only nothing could ever be right with me, Samantha thought. No amount of goodness could change what she was or the undead life she lived because of the cruelty of men.

"Goodbye, Detective," she said and closed the door on him. Hopefully forever.

Chapter 7

The steel chains binding Meghan to the hooks in the cement wall were cold against her skin. The wall was rough against her body. The sicko liked to keep her naked, her feet barely touching the ground.

Meghan pulled at the chains feebly, weak from the need to feed and the daylight that snuck in through the window at the end of the day, searing her skin. She couldn't recall how many times that sunlight had popped in to inflict its punishment. Had it been two or three days? she wondered.

It was becoming hard to focus due to her waning strength and the fear that touched her during the long bouts of being alone and confined. Fear that would roar to life once he'd come back to play his demented games.

She should have known better than to go with the old man. She'd thought he'd be an easy conquest. The weak usually were.

Only he'd turned the tables on her the moment they'd left the club.

Meghan hadn't known what hit her. All she knew was that a sudden explosion of pain had brought her to her knees before she lost consciousness.

During her captivity, she'd learned that the perverted ol' bastard had used a Taser on her. She still bore burn marks from the last time. Which was not good. She wasn't healing anymore because she was too debilitated.

If the old man took any more of her blood, or played too many more of his sadistic little games, she wouldn't survive.

Maybe that was for the best, Meghan thought. This wasn't the kind of life she'd envisioned for herself. She'd been hoping for college in the city followed by a 9-to-5-rush-home-to-the-suburbs kind of life.

Thanks to Blake that would never be. *Blake.* That skanky-assed punk vampire.

Meghan swore that if there was one thing she'd do before she met her end—the second time—it would be to see that Blake got his for what he'd done to her.

The creak of the door alerted her to the old man's arrival and thoughts of revenge were driven away by dread. Meghan pulled at her chains, but it accomplished nothing. He smiled at her foolish attempts, and picked up a scalpel.

Meghan bit back a whimper. She hated when he used the scalpel, but she refused to let him know. Her pride was the only thing she had left. Despite her intentions, however, she couldn't control her involuntary flinch as the old man ran the flat edge of the blade along her midsection.

"Good afternoon, my dear," he said, bringing his face so close to hers that she had no choice but to look into his cold blue eyes.

"What's so good about it?" She jangled the chains with what little strength she had left.

"It's your last."

Peter holstered his Glock and stepped away from the wounded teenager. Given the extent of the young man's injuries, he probably wouldn't survive.

Peter'd had no time for guilt or second-guessing. If he hadn't shot back, he'd be the one bleeding to death on the floor of the warehouse. And if the teen had gotten away, he would have been free to hurt someone else. The way he'd shot those kids in front of the Artemis Shelter.

Peter took another look around the gang hangout. A few tables and chairs. Beat-up secondhand sofas clustered in front of a state-of-the-art plasma television. Some clubhouse.

"Sorry, Detective. We lost the other suspect about two blocks away." The officer was winded as he spoke, a testament to the chase he'd given.

"The one you shot outside is dead. He's one of the perps you were trying to find," the second officer said.

Two down and one on the loose. And with one perp dead and the other likely to expire, Peter would be up before a review board in the morning. Taking his gun out of his holster, he held it out to the young black officer. She hesitated, but he waved it at her. "You know the routine."

She took the gun and nodded. "I'll hold it until CSU finishes."

"I'd appreciate that. Did you get a good look at the third perp?"

Her answer was interrupted by the growing wail of an ambulance siren. It arrived in a rush of activity as the EMTs tried to stabilize the wounded perp.

CSU arrived minutes after that, as well as his captain. Peter appreciated the older man coming down to the scene to offer his support. "Captain," he said with a respectful nod.

"You okay, Daly?" The older man reached into his jacket pocket, eased out a pack of cigarettes and offered Peter one.

"Sorry, I don't smoke."

Captain Fitzgerald smiled and slipped the pack back into his pocket. "Neither do I, but it helps some of the men, you know."

Peter doubted a smoke would help him deal with the fact that he'd killed one person and critically wounded another. He watched the ambulance pull away, and then turned his attention to the CSU people who were busy taking photos and gathering evidence.

His captain tracked his gaze and said, "Did you have any other choice?"

Peter replayed that moment in his mind, going over each step the perp had taken. Rewinding the scene in his brain again and again, but no matter what, the outcome was the same. "Perp was firing at us. He had Rodriguez and White pinned behind their car. I had no choice."

"And the second one?"

"Firing from the doorway. They weren't going to stop, Captain." The two teens hadn't stopped the other night when they'd shot those kids and they'd had no qualms about trying to add a few cops to their growing pile of bodies. The prints they'd found on the van had led them here, to young men who had rap sheets already pages long.

"You'll have to give a full report in the morning, Daly. Make sure you've got your facts straight."

"Yes, sir," he said and motioned to the two uniformed officers answering CSU's questions. "They'll be able to confirm everything, Captain. I did it all by the book."

The captain grasped his shoulder in a gesture meant to reassure. "I have no doubt about it, Daly. You always do everything according to regulation."

Peter nodded, but the comfort from the older man's words wasn't enough. Following the rules only made it a little easier to deal with the fact that he'd killed two people. The day that it became easy, he'd turn in his shield.

But for today, just as he had told his captain, he'd had no choice.

Chapter 8

Samantha, Diego and Esperanza swept through the crowd in the Blood Bank, hoping to find Meghan. It had been nearly a week since her disappearance and they still didn't have a clue as to where she'd gone.

Esperanza thought the young vamp had finally decided to sacrifice herself to the light she loved so much. With a vampire Meghan's age, it wouldn't take that long. Just a few hours and she would be dead, drained of her life force by the sun's rays. Another few hours and all that would be left was a big pile of ash.

Diego refused to believe Meghan would do something so drastic. He had always been understanding of Meghan's moods, urging the others to remember what they'd been like at twenty-one.

Samantha couldn't remember being twenty-one, at least not with the possibility of the carefree existence so many modern women enjoyed. At twenty-one she'd been working hard at the tavern her parents had once owned. By twenty-three she'd been married, enduring the beatings of her husband. By twenty-five, she'd been dead and reborn in her current state, enduring the torture inflicted by her condition and by the vampire who'd sired her.

She had never known what it was to be like Meghan.

"She hasn't been back here, you know." Blake leaned his arms on the edge of her booth and peered down at her.

Samantha turned and glanced up at the punk vamp. There was an edge of concern there. "How do you know?"

With a shrug, he came around and sat beside her. "Been looking for her myself."

She was surprised, since Blake generally didn't care about anything other than himself. "Why?"

With another shrug, he said, "I liked Meghan. She made me laugh, when she wasn't all wonky about being human again."

"She was young, Blake. Too young."

"So was I," he said angrily, surprising her. "So were you. And unlike Diego or his little chit, I'm assuming you didn't choose to become this way."

No, Samantha thought. Becoming a vampire had been the furthest thing from her mind on the night she'd died.

New Orleans, 1861

"Is there anything I can do?"

Samantha brought a cup of tea to Mrs. Danvers, who was seated in a rocker by her son's cradle, watching her husband pace back and forth. From the look on the doctor's face, he didn't like the way the illness was progressing.

Despite Dr. Danvers' best efforts, his baby's fever had been rising steadily. Now the boy's breathing had grown labored.

"I know it's late—" He quickly dashed off a note. "Please take this to the apothecary on the corner near the convent of the Ursuline nuns. He'll still be open and able to make this medicine for you."

The Danvers family had been more than kind to Samantha in the months since Ryder Latimer had secured her a position in their New Orleans household after the death of her husband. She was willing to help them in any way she could.

Samantha shot a quick look at the paper and hurried from the room. She paused only long enough to grab a shawl and check her purse for cash.

The walk wasn't far, just a dozen or so blocks, but a low-lying fog blanketed the ground. It whirled and eddied past her long skirts. Even with the shawl, the damp chill reached into her, making the hairs on the back of her neck stand on end.

Or was it something else?

Was that a footfall behind her? She stopped and looked, but there was nothing except shifting fog.

Wrapping the shawl tighter around herself, she kept a fist clutched to the cloth as she continued on. But once more, the sound came. This time, Samantha didn't stop. She increased her pace and rushed around a corner.

Holding her breath, she waited against the wall of a building but no one appeared. Telling herself that it was just her imagination, she turned—and found her way blocked by a tall man in a long black cloak and hat.

"Excuse me, sir." She tried to pass by him, but he shifted to bar her. The hairs on the back of her neck rose once more and she stepped back. He followed her. She had only once choice.

Samantha ran, as fast as she could. But like before, when she looked behind her there was no one there.

She held a hand to her midsection as she tried to catch her

breath. She had detoured a few blocks from the main street, into a part of the French Quarter that was not well-traveled at this time of night.

Merde. The Danvers baby waited at home for the medicine she was supposed to fetch. Concern drove away her fear. She turned back toward the convent.

She had gone only a block when footsteps chased behind her once more. She didn't stop. She had something to accomplish. She would not let unwarranted fear keep her from the important task. The sounds behind her were just…

A hand covered her mouth as a man's strong arm wrapped around her waist. Struggling against his hold, she kicked and rocked from side to side. But he easily picked her up and dragged her into an alley.

Samantha had little doubt what awaited her, but she wasn't about to give in. She bit down hard on the palm clamped against her mouth. The man shifted his hold, but not long enough for her to scream. He quickly covered her mouth again and roughly shoved her against a wall. Her head connected with the bricks. She saw stars and shook her head to clear her vision.

When she was finally able to see the face before her, horror choked her. Her assailant was not a man. He was a demon.

His eyes were a bright unnatural green and long pointed fangs extended well beyond his upper lip. "Do you like what you see, *cherie?*"

He moved his free hand to the neckline of her dress and gave a vicious yank, ripping the fabric to reveal her chemise. With a second yank, he tore the fine lawn to expose her breasts.

Samantha increased her struggles, kicking and pulling, but the demon's hold was too strong. His grip on her mouth was unyielding, making it hard to breathe. She clasped her legs tight together, but he was too powerful.

With his leg tucked between hers, he quickly made rags of her underthings and roughly opened her with his fingers. Then he shoved himself into her cruelly.

Samantha cried out in pain. It only brought a smile to her attacker's face.

"It's big isn't it, *cherie.*" The force of his thrusts picked her up off the ground and ripped apart her insides.

Her tears made the demon laugh.

Anger filled her—against this violation and all the others she'd suffered in silence at her husband's hands. She bit down. Hard enough to break the skin of his hand, and she kept biting even as he smacked her head against the wall.

"Like to bite, do you?"

The glow in his eyes intensified and his fangs grew. Almost as if he were excited by her struggles.

It made her hesitate. A hesitation that cost her her life.

The demon turned her head to the side, bared her neck and drove his fangs in deep.

Pain seared through her. She screamed and screamed, but no one heard her. No one helped.

"That's a bitch, love. I'm sorry." Samantha shook her head to drive away the memories. Though her recounting tonight had been matter-of-fact, she'd not yet been able to remember her turning dispassionately. And ever since the detective— Peter—had touched her scars, the first person to do so since they'd healed, memories of her pain and loss had been too close to the surface. Close enough that she'd needed to share them with Blake, a virtual stranger.

Blake's commiseration was…unexpected. Propping her head in one hand, she examined him as if for the first time. He was a handsome young man, all the punk trappings notwithstanding. And tonight there was an unexpected sense of connection between them.

"What were you before?" she asked.

Blake motioned to Samantha's drink, which sat untouched on the table. "Mind if I have a sip? I'm a little low on cash tonight."

After she nodded, Blake took a drink. "Ah, only the finest for Diego, our little lordling, and his friends. That's the way it always is. Even in my small village in Wales."

She hadn't known he was Welsh. His accent was more Cockney than anything else. "Is that where it happened? In Wales?"

"There was a rich man in my town. He had a penchant for young men and we were poor." He paused and took another small taste of the blood, as if he were sampling a fine brandy. Maybe in the vampire world, it was. As he continued, the Cockney twang lessened and a rich, more cultured accent replaced it. "It had been an especially hard season. Crops were bad and my family was hungry."

"You went to him," Samantha said when he hesitated.

The pain on his face was unsettling. "What good was my virtue when the little ones' stomachs were empty? So I went to him and he paid me. I became his favorite. One day he showed me his true face and then…he turned me."

He slugged back the rest of the drink and angrily slammed the glass down on the table.

Samantha laid a comforting hand on his. "I'm sorry. I've misjudged you."

"What of your family? A beautiful woman like you had to have a husband."

She had never told anyone before, but she couldn't hold back after what Blake had just recounted. "My husband had been killed in a poker game."

"I'm sorry."

"Don't be," she replied harshly. "He used to beat me. He killed our baby, so I was…relieved. Finally free."

"Free." Blake's gaze was filled with yearning. "The only time I've ever felt that way was with Meghan. She made me feel free again. I didn't want to lose her."

"Is that why you sired her?"

"Yes. And you? Have you ever turned anyone?"

An odd combination of guilt and relief swept over her. "Only one. After my husband died, someone befriended me."

"He was the one you turned? Did you care for him?"

She had cared for him, but not in the way Blake thought. "Ryder Latimer was a doctor. He'd helped me when I lost my baby and then after, when my husband Elias died."

"How did he help?"

Samantha suddenly felt exposed before the punk vampire.

"Samantha." The understanding in his voice convinced her to finish her story.

"Ryder had a friend whose wife had just had a child. Ryder arranged for his friend to hire me as his housekeeper and it was wonderful. The Danvers family was kind and treated me well."

"Unfortunately, you didn't live happily ever after."

"Is there ever a happily ever after?"

An empty silence followed, as if the telling of their stories had drained them of words. Blake signaled the waitress for another round of drinks, and then proposed a toast.

"To finding Meghan," he said.

"To finding Meghan." Although with each day that passed, Samantha grew more doubtful that they ever would.

After taking a bracing sip of the human blood, which tasted as if it had just been drawn, she said, "Do you remember anything about the man with Meghan?"

Blake shook his head. "Only that he was carbon-dated."

"Carbon-dated? As in—"

"Fossilized."

"In English. Please, Blake." She suspected Blake's concept of old could range anywhere from thirty to eighty.

"Gray hair. Fiftyish? I don't right remember. Human, I think. All buttoned-up and proper. Does that ring a bell for you?" he asked as he finished the drink.

Samantha racked her brains for anyone, either vamp or human, that matched the description, but could think of no one. "Not at all, but maybe Diego and Esperanza know."

"Yeah, well. You can fill them in about Meghan's friend. In the meantime, I'm going to take another look around. I intend to find her."

With a wave, Blake sauntered away, his cocky swagger and good looks making a few female heads turn.

Normally Samantha would sit and wait for Diego and Esperanza to return, but she was filled with nervous energy from her discussion. Rising from the bench, she slipped into the crowd. An older man was likely to stick out like a sore thumb. And as for "buttoned-up and proper," in a crowd of black, leather and chains, that kind of dress was like a neon sign.

Which made her wonder just why Meghan had gone with the old man.

Samantha worked her way through the throng and along the edges. Until she ran into Diego and Esperanza, who were huddled in a deserted corner, their search for Meghan apparently forgotten.

She tried not to look, but failed miserably.

Diego fondled Esperanza's breasts and his leg was tucked tight between her thighs. Esperanza rode him that way, relieving her need for the moment. Her head was thrown back in passion, but then she sensed Samantha's presence. Esperanza lowered her head, met Samantha's gaze, and transformed. Then, she sank her fangs into Diego's neck.

The power of that bite sent a wave of sexual awakening through Samantha. A yearning to share her life with someone besides the women and children at the shelter and her vampire friends. Someone who could love her like Diego and Esperanza loved one another. Someone strong and honorable like…

She hurried away, needing to put distance between herself and her friends. Between herself and thoughts of the detective she couldn't drive from her mind.

Back at the booth, she grabbed the shot glass with what was left of her drink and with shaky hands, knocked back the last dregs of blood. As she placed the glass down, something caught her attention.

Blake, heading into one of the back rooms. Who had he been with? Someone older?

She tried to slip beyond the curtain but was stopped by the vampire who ran the private area. "No one comes back here alone. You know the rules."

"Blake—"

"Had some company. Willing company." He inclined his head in the direction of the main room and she stepped back beyond the boundary of the curtain like a coach passenger being chased out of First Class.

With her friends otherwise occupied, there was only one thing left to do—go home.

Home. Only, even with all the people waiting there for her, home suddenly didn't seem quite so welcoming.

Chapter 9

For the second time in just over a week, he was at the Artemis Shelter and calling himself a fool.

The review board that morning had cleared him in the shootings. Peter hadn't expected anything else, but it was the first time he'd ever killed anyone in all the years he had been a cop. Inside, there was a dull ache that refused to go away.

The first perp had been only fifteen. The second one, who died on the operating table, had just turned sixteen. Guilt had eaten away at Peter all night and long past the review board's verdict. It made little difference that ballistics had identified one of the guns as the weapon that killed the three teenagers the other night. No matter that the fingerprints taken from the two dead suspects had confirmed one of them as the shooter. The youngest.

An eye for an eye, the Bible said. Peter tried to find comfort in that and in the fact that he had prevented others from becoming the boys' victims in the future.

He didn't like violence, but sometimes it was necessary, he thought, leaning on the bullet-riddled fender of his car. And he didn't want to think about how the recent violence in his life kept pulling him toward Samantha Turner.

She might be in danger. The third perp, a local seventeen-year-old with a long rap sheet was still on the loose. If he thought Samantha or anyone else in the shelter might have seen him, he might come back to silence them. That was the reason why Peter stood on Samantha's doorstep. He needed to let her know.

At least, that was the reason he gave himself.

The comfort he experienced around Samantha Turner was…unwise. Possibly wishful thinking. His wife had shown him the same understanding at first. Then she had demonstrated her true colors by betraying him.

But Samantha was a different kind of creature. He sensed that about her. And he sensed that she needed…something. He didn't know what. This fascination with the enigmatic head of the shelter was absurd.

But the temptation to find out more about her called to him.

The house was quiet. The women she sheltered were at work, their children at school. Sofia was in class at a nearby college where Samantha had managed to secure a grant for her.

Samantha was smiling when she answered the knock at the door.

"You should smile more often. You're beautiful when you smile."

The detective's words wiped the joy from her face. "And the rest of the time? How do I look then?"

"Sad, but still beautiful," he said. "May I come in?"

She was tempted to tell him to go away, but there was something about him this morning that tugged at her heart-strings, reawakening the emotions she'd run from last night. "Come in, Detective. It's rather late for breakfast, but—"

"I'm not really hungry, Samantha. And it's Peter, remember?"

She had the leisure of examining him as he stepped in. His face was a little haggard, as if he hadn't slept well. There was a small cut just above his brow. "Peter." She motioned for him to make himself comfortable in the front parlor.

Politely, he indicated she should sit first. She chose the couch and was a little surprised when he sat down beside her, invading her space. She shied away, uneasy with his physical presence.

"Do you want me to move?" Peter pointed to the chair beside the sofa.

"No, it's okay. Really. So what can I do for you today?"

He laid two photographs on the coffee table. "Do you recognize these young men?"

Samantha didn't need more than a brief look. The teenagers' faces had been etched in her memory. "They're dead."

Peter nodded. "Do you recognize them?"

Samantha touched the photos as if by doing so she could touch their spirits. What had they felt when released from their lives here on Earth? Had it been relief or regret? Or had it not even mattered to two souls with no regard for so precious a gift? "They were so young. Who killed them?"

Peter's hands were clenched into tight fists. His body was tense. She didn't need for him to tell her. It was there for her to see. His pain. His guilt. His confusion.

His emotions tore into her, making her feel more than she had in too long.

"I'm sorry, Peter." She tried to cradle his cheek, but he

yanked away from her touch. She recognized that defense all too well. Grasping her hands in her lap to keep from reaching for him again, she said, "Sometimes people deserve to die."

A cold hard fact some would say she was cruel to hold to. But it was what she believed. Her husband Elias had deserved to die. If she hadn't been such a coward, taken matters into her own hands, her child would be alive. And maybe, just maybe, she wouldn't be the way she was today.

They sat for long minutes, each trapped in their own personal hell, and then he laid his hand over hers. She didn't pull away.

"Did you kill your husband?"

She let out a strangled laugh. "In my dreams sometimes. But no, I didn't. He was killed in a card game."

"And his death set you free?"

"I thought that it would, only it didn't."

Peter saw something in her face he hadn't expected to see. There were more layers to this woman than the few he'd peeled away so far. Layers that went deep, ones that maybe he didn't want to disturb. Perhaps it was this unknown quality that kept bringing him back, and made him want to share. "When my wife left, I hated her. After the divorce, I felt free…for all of about two seconds."

"And then?" she asked, her hand still beneath his, but trembling, as if it cost her a great deal to allow his touch.

"Like you I realized it hadn't. Other people can't set you free. That comes from within."

Slowly she twined her fingers with his and his heart did a funky drum roll in the middle of his chest. The guys at the precinct would get a real kick out of this. Big tough detective melting inside from a simple touch. But in that touch was the promise of so much more. More than he had thought possible after his wife's betrayal.

But that promise brought fear, because he wasn't sure this—whatever was between them—was a good thing. And fear for her, because she wasn't safe from the last suspect.

Reluctant to break contact with her, he fumbled with the last photo, which he placed on the table beside the other two. "This is the third suspect. He may come back here if he thinks you've fingered him."

"May I keep that photo? Show it to the others in the shelter." There was little concern in her voice.

"You need to be careful, Samantha. He may be young, but he's dangerous."

"I know, Peter. I can take care of things, as can the other women here. We're used to dealing with violence." Her smile transformed her face. "Besides, I suspect we'll be seeing our share of you around here until this guy is caught. Right?"

Peter chuckled, relieved by the unexpected invitation into her world. Wanting to keep the moment light, because he sensed she'd had too much darkness in her life, he said, "Only if you promise to make me more of those square sugary things."

She gave a quick laugh. "So it is true, then."

"What's true?"

"That the way to a cop's heart *is* with a donut."

Blake was missing.

He hadn't been to the club in days. Totally unlike the socially needy vampire whose undead life revolved around the Blood Bank and its occupants. Not to mention that Blake had said he intended to find Meghan. Maybe he had. Maybe that's why he was missing now.

"Are there any others gone besides Blake and Meghan?" Samantha asked Diego.

He gave an elegant shrug. "I've tried to ask around, but no one wants to be involved. They have their own groups to protect and don't want to become mired in our problems."

"*Our* problems? Since when is Blake—"

"Our problem? *Amiga,* most of the others would have willingly ripped his throat out if not for the punishment that might bring from me."

"Maybe they ran off together? After all, Blake sired her. Maybe she finally realized just how wonderful a thing that was." Esperanza was aflutter as she proposed this theory. She slipped her arm through Diego's and smiled at him lovingly.

Diego patted her arm, but met Samantha's gaze across the small width of their table. He knew she held no love for the vampire who'd sired her. He'd been cruel and savage, forcing her to do things that, to this day, Samantha regretted.

"Maybe we should talk to someone." As soon as she suggested it she wished she hadn't. Who could a vampire call when they needed help? That had been the human within speaking, forgetting that no one would wish to help someone like her.

"Your mortal friend has been hanging around too much, *querida.* He's making you forget what you are."

It had only been a few days since Peter began dropping by the shelter, presumably to keep an eye on things until the third suspect in the shooting was captured. He visited in the early morning before his shift and they shared a cup of coffee. At night, if she glanced out the parlor window, she'd see his car parked outside. Peter would be sitting behind the wheel, sipping a cup of coffee or reading the paper.

It was…comforting. A word she had not ever been able to use to describe her relationship with a man. There was a gentleness about him, even though she knew he was capable of violence. And there was pain in him as well. She'd felt it when he'd told her about killing the two suspects and about his ex-wife's betrayal.

She saw it when he gazed at the children during breakfast. His yearning made her wonder why he hadn't remarried and had children of his own. But she wouldn't ask, just like she knew he wouldn't ask again about her husband. Because the questions would lead to an intimacy far greater than the two of them could ever share.

Now, as they ordered shots from the waitress, Diego repeated his warning, "You can never be what he wants, Samantha."

There was no point in arguing. He was right. So she said, "What do you think happened to Blake and Meghan?"

Esperanza, still flustered and romantic, repeated her earlier suggestion. "They've gone off together. I'm sure of it. Meghan finally came to her senses."

Diego forced a smile. "I'm sure that's what happened, *mi amor*," he said. But as he dropped a kiss on Esperanza's forehead, Samantha saw his concern.

Something had happened to their friends and it seemed like they would have to go at it all alone to find out what.

Chapter 10

When Blake woke, all he could remember was pain.

From the first sharp blast that had weakened his knees, to the second that had knocked him out. When he roused, he'd found himself chained to a wall, and the pain had only gotten worse.

The old dude he'd seen with Meghan had stood before Blake, wearing a white lab jacket, something long and shiny sticking out of his pocket. A hypodermic Blake had realized, as he was poked, prodded, and sliced open slowly so Mr. Mad Scientist could use him as a lab rat until Blake passed out from the torment.

But now, as consciousness returned, he realized he was not bound. He fought to rise from the cold cement floor. That was when he saw Meghan. Or what was left of her.

Too weak to stand, he dragged himself to her nearly lifeless body. Even with his own weakness, he could hear the slight, uneven thrum of her heart.

When he reached her, he sat back against the rough cinder block wall and somehow picked her up and held her close. "Meghan, baby. Can you hear me? It's Blake." She just lay limp in his arms. Her skin was as cold as ice and slightly damp with the sweat that said her body was failing.

He couldn't let her die. "Meghan," he said again, more forcefully. "You need to feed."

Again there was no response. Blake cradled her tighter and sliced open one of his wrists with his nails. It would weaken him further to give some of his life's blood to her, but otherwise, he would lose her.

Bright red drops welled along the slash he'd made and he brought his bleeding wrist to her mouth.

At first there was no reaction as his blood oozed onto her lips and into her mouth. Patiently he continued to hold her, murmuring soft words of encouragement, until finally, her mouth closed over his wrist. Little by little the pull grew stronger. Her body warmed beside him. Because he, too, was weak, his body chilled with the power she took from him until he was almost too feeble to hold her.

But by then she had roused and looked up at him, her eyes haunted as she fed until she realized he could no longer give any more. She eased away from him, her lips stained with his blood, and then she surprised him. She leaned close and kissed him, let him lick what was left of his offering from her lips.

"Why?" she asked.

Blake could barely move, debilitated by the experiments done on him and Meghan's feeding. He struggled to focus. "Ah, love. Because I couldn't bear to lose you."

He waited for Meghan's usual tirade about how she hated him. How she wanted him dead for siring her. Instead she held him tight to her breasts, like she might cradle a baby. "Rest, Blake. We need our strength to survive this."

Then she kissed him again, or at least he thought she did as he released himself to the rest that would rebuild his strength.

"I don't think this is a good idea anymore, Peter," Samantha said, her stance rigid as she stood in the doorway to the shelter.

"Excuse me?" Was that animosity in her voice? He thought they had reached some kind of peace. During the time they'd spent together over the last few days, he'd sensed a change between them, a shift that said their relationship had become more personal.

"It's been almost a week now and there's no sign of your suspect. It seems he's turned his attention elsewhere and the women here are uneasy with a man around."

You mean you're uneasy around me, he thought. After an initial cold shoulder from some of the women, they had warmed up to him. And the kids…How he loved playing with the kids first thing in the morning. He had even helped some of the older ones with last-minute homework.

But she was right about one thing. The perp had probably left the neighborhood. Peter had tracked down every known hideout and acquaintance, but the searches had yielded nothing. Luckily a grand jury had thought there was enough evidence to issue an indictment. That didn't end the case, but with an arrest warrant issued, he didn't need to be at the shelter every day.

"You may be right—"

"I'm glad you see it that way. So if you'll excuse me." She

began to close the door, but Peter grabbed it to keep it from shutting in his face.

"The perp's probably long gone and I certainly don't want to upset anybody. So how about we go for breakfast around the corner?"

There was a dismayed look on her face. "I-I-I don't think you understood. I'd rather you not come by anymore."

So he *did* get to her. Good. But he wanted her to admit it. He cradled her cheek and was pleased when she didn't pull away. For days he'd wondered what it would be like to touch her, to feel her creamy skin beneath his fingers. He wasn't disappointed. She was as soft and smooth as she looked, even if a bit cold.

"You can't keep running, Samantha. Or hiding behind the women in the shelter."

"I'm not hiding." She tightened her lips into a thin line of exasperation.

"Aren't you?" He slipped his thumb over her lips, needing to feel them, even if only like this.

"Peter, please—"

He didn't give her a chance to finish. He brought his lips to hers and didn't let up until her resistance faded and she finally kissed him back.

A cough made him step away. Sofia stood behind Samantha, a broad smile on her face. She winked at him while addressing Samantha. "There's a call for you. It's Diego."

The satisfying flush of color on Samantha's cheeks faded. "I need to take this call," she said and hurried away.

Sofia surprised him by saying, "Don't worry. Diego's never been around and as far as I know, she's never made him beignets."

That brought a smile to his face. "Tell Samantha I'll be back tonight."

"Will do, Detective. Be careful out there," Sofia said, an earnest tone to her voice.

"Why, Ms. Sofia. Might you actually be worried about me?"

Sofia rolled her eyes and chuckled. As she shut the door in his face, she said, "I'm worried about what I will do to you if you hurt Samantha."

Peter turned on his heel and walked down the steps, almost whistling as he imagined coming back later that night and continuing where they had left off.

With him kissing her.

Diego was frantic.

Although it had been nearly two weeks since Meghan's disappearance and going on a week since Blake had likewise vanished, Diego had refused to believe Meghan would not return.

And so he had convinced Esperanza to go with him to the Blood Bank last night. Annoyed that Diego continued to be concerned about the young vampire, Esperanza had refused to leave the booth with him when he went to search the club. Instead, she chose to remain there, pouting petulantly and sipping a glass of the Blood Bank's finest.

That was the last Diego had seen of her. He had returned to their lair—a posh apartment on New York's Central Park West—thinking she'd tired of sitting alone. The entire night had gone by with no sign of his lover.

"The sun grows stronger every minute, Samantha."

She stared out the window of the front parlor as she listened to Diego on the phone. "I know, Diego. Did she mention anything last night?"

"Only that I seemed to care more for Meghan than I did for her, which is absurd. But you know how jealous Esperanza can be."

Samantha racked her brains, but could think of no other place where Esperanza would go besides the Artemis Shelter. The other vampires at the club—a company of a dozen or more—had little patience for others' problems.

And they clearly had a problem. First Meghan, then Blake and now Esperanza. Who would be next?

"I'm going back to the club," Diego said. "Someone has to have seen something."

"You're thinking with your heart and not your head, Diego. You can't go back."

"But—"

"Whatever is going on is tied to the Blood Bank. Until we know what's happening, it's best to stay away from there." Her mind raced as she imagined what someone could want with three vampires.

Nothing good.

There was a long silence on the telephone line followed by a harsh sigh. "What do I do in the meantime?"

A good question. They had nothing to go on. It wasn't like she was going to suddenly go Nancy Drew and start investigating.

"We wait," she said. When Diego protested she added, "Just a day or two. It will give us time to think about what's happened. Try to get all the facts so that when we go back to the club, we won't be sitting ducks, waiting to be taken as well."

As Samantha hung up, she wondered if it wasn't time to ask someone to investigate. But as quickly as that thought came, she drove it away. There was no one who would help someone like her. Not even Peter despite his obvious interest in her. And her fascination with him.

No matter how hard she tried, she couldn't forget his kiss. That wonderful hopeful first kiss. And last.

Not even this situation with her missing friends could change the facts. She shouldn't get involved with him for so many reasons. First, she was a vampire. Couples-to-be could deal with lots of differences but undead and mortal wasn't a difference you could ignore or agree to disagree about.

Second, as gentle as he'd been around the occupants of the shelter, she knew his capability for violence. He'd even killed in the line of duty.

Violence was a part of her nature as much as it was a part of his, but she had resisted violence for many years. She would continue to do so. It wasn't what she wanted in life. She wanted a peaceful existence. One without the complications of missing friends and a mortal man who made her want more than she could have. Such longing could only bring pain. A life with Peter was an impossibility because she didn't have a life of her own to offer him.

Chapter 11

Blake woke to the sound of footsteps and something being dragged. Alerting Meghan, who had been asleep in his arms, he walked them back to the furthest corner of the cell. Out of reach of the cattle prod Mr. Mad Scientist occasionally used, but not beyond the range of the Taser. Still, their little rebellion was worth it to make the old man's life difficult. He seemed to respect that kind of spunk, Blake had discovered. Now even Meghan was getting a little spirit, which was a relief. If they were to survive this, they had to be in it together. Him, Meghan—and now Esperanza.

He hadn't wanted to give up her name, but he hadn't had much choice. At least not after the cut that had nearly split him open. Any more damage and he wouldn't have been able to heal, even with a feeding from another vampire.

Funny thing really, the truth about vampires compared to Hollywood myths and legends. It didn't take a stake or decapitation. They didn't burst into flame and ash at the very first rays of sunlight. Blake had even heard stories of a very old vampire who'd had his heart cut out, but survived long enough to get it back from the unsuspecting vampire slayer and eventually heal.

Healing being one of the wondrous gifts that came with their nocturnal existence.

But he wouldn't have been able to heal if Mr. Mad Scientist had continued with the wounds he seemed to love inflicting. Plus, Blake couldn't leave Meghan alone to suffer at the hands of the lunatic who'd taken them.

So he'd betrayed Esperanza, and then Samantha, but with a reason. Diego—the strongest of them all—was bound to come after his lover and the woman who'd been his best friend for nearly a century. With Diego in the mix, maybe they could escape their captor and the pair of goons he kept around to assist him. Humans one and all only…

There was something about the old man that wasn't quite right. As if he wasn't totally human.

It wasn't like the clean hum of power that came from another vampire. It was more like the snap and crackle of static—erratic and untrustworthy.

Whatever it was, it made Blake wonder if the good doctor wasn't what he seemed. He certainly lacked humanity, otherwise he wouldn't be torturing and maiming them like science experiments.

As the sounds grew closer, Meghan trembled. He took hold of her hand. "Don't let him see that you're afraid."

She gripped his hand tightly as their captor came into view, two of his goons dragging a lifeless Esperanza. Tasers in hand, they opened the door of the cell, tossed Esperanza inside, and then immediately locked the cell once again.

"You lied to me, Blake. I don't like liars." The old scientist took one of the Tasers from his minion. With a dismissive wave of his hand, he said to them, "Go wait for me in my office."

"I don't know what you mean. I didn't lie."

"You said she would be stronger." The scientist motioned to Esperanza, who lay sprawled on the cement floor.

Fear snapped to life in Blake's gut. Esperanza was too pale. Too still. Maybe he was too far away, or maybe she was too weak, but he couldn't feel her power. He didn't understand how that could be unless...

"She's much older than Meghan and me. She should be stronger."

"Feed her, Blake. Like you did with Meghan because I'm not done with her yet."

Blake wanted to refuse, but the old man picked up the Taser, making it clear what the punishment would be if Blake didn't comply.

Behind him, Meghan stood up straighter. "We're not afraid of you."

Edward Sloan was impressed with the way the young blond vampire had finally decided to stand up to him. He admired her spirit. But as much as he admired it, he wouldn't hesitate to destroy her, if it meant finding the missing pieces of the puzzle, the one that would be a cure for his illness. Luckily, some of the pieces were standing right here.

Soon he would have answers. He had to. The mutated cells in his body were barely under control. Only regular transfusions, which he required more and more often, were of any use.

The vampires would yield the cure. So he needed

Esperanza up and about, since Blake and Meghan weren't up to further experimentation yet.

"Feed her." He once again motioned to Esperanza's still body.

As Blake inched toward Esperanza, the lean muscles of his body rippled. He was a magnificent animal.

Edward had watched the two vampires over the last week or so. He'd been entranced by the caring Blake had shown and Meghan's reaction to it. It was a pity he couldn't keep them as lab rats to see just how things were between vampires. How they mated and whether they bore others of their kind.

Edward drew closer to the cell, intent on watching Blake feed the older vampire. But Blake paused and laid his hand on her body. "She's gone. You've killed her."

"That's not possible," Edward replied. "You said she would be—"

The young vampire launched himself at the bars of the cell, grabbing Edward. "You bastard. You killed her."

Edward pulled the trigger on the Taser. Blake's body recoiled as electricity surged through him, but he still held onto Edward, all the time screaming and cursing.

Edward struggled and called out for his assistants, who came running. One man fired off another Taser blast, which did little more than the first. The second man, seeing that the Taser wasn't working, grabbed the cattle prod and shoved it onto Blake's midsection.

Blake jerked back and finally started to lose his grip. A second jab had him dropping to his knees. When the guard went for a third prod, Edward stopped him. "We can't afford to lose this one yet."

As Blake held onto the cell bars for support, Edward placed a well-heeled shoe on Blake's chest and shoved harshly, sending the vampire sprawling back onto the floor. He lay there, his body jerking from the Taser's electricity. Large reddish burn marks were rising on his body.

Meghan moved to Blake's side. "Leave him and go to the woman. Feed her," Edward commanded, his tone cold and brooking no disagreement.

Meghan shot Blake a woeful glance before proceeding to Esperanza's side. With a fingernail, she sliced open the middle of her forearm. Blood flowed freely and Meghan slipped her uninjured arm beneath the woman's shoulders. Gently, like a mother urging her newborn infant to suckle, Meghan held her bloodied arm to Esperanza's mouth. Over and over again she let the blood drip into it, until it was apparent to all that the other vampire wasn't responding. She was gone.

"Stop wasting that blood," Edward snapped in irritation. "Feed your boyfriend. He's going to need all the strength he has for what I've got in store for him."

Meghan scurried over to Blake and cradled him close. The vampire woke slowly and latched on to Meghan's arm.

Edward could almost sense the strength flowing from one to the other. With some of their blood running in his veins, he could feel the growing heat of their bodies. Blood lust would be replaced by sexual lust. Soon, once Blake had satisfied one need, they would go to work satisfying another.

Snapping his fingers at his two guards, who stood transfixed watching the display, he prodded them to move on. He was eager to return to his office. Once there, he'd replace some of his own contaminated blood with Esperanza's. And while he waited for that new blood to energize his body, he could view the two lusty vampires thanks to the camera mounted in the corner of the cell.

He grew excited thinking about that and about fetching himself the new vampire Esperanza had claimed would be strong enough for what Edward wanted. Samantha, the vampire Blake had previously mentioned.

He only hoped his new prey would prove more interesting and long-lived than the last.

Chapter 12

The phone sat in the middle of his desk and every time it rang he hoped it would be her. But three days after she'd closed the door on him, she hadn't called.

With two of the perps dead and the last one seemingly gone for good, there was no reason for him to go by the shelter. But he had gone each night, detouring uptown before he headed to his empty apartment.

He hadn't seen Samantha, though he'd sat in the car waiting like a hopeful schoolboy for any sign of her. Wishing he could find a reason to march up the steps of the shelter and knock on the door. He hadn't been able to get her out of his mind no matter how hard he tried.

The lady packed a wallop. That was for sure.

The phone rang.

He grabbed it. "Daly, here."

It was a detective from another precinct, asking for information on a suspect. After the phone call, Peter forced his attention back to the case sitting on his desk—a young woman who had been killed in a carjacking after taking the wrong exit off the FDR Drive.

But as he examined the photos of the victim, all he could see was Samantha's jet-black hair and crystalline blue eyes. With an annoyed sigh, he closed the folder and reminded himself that he wasn't the kind of man to sit around and wait.

He was used to taking action when he had to and, in his book, it had definitely reached that point. He couldn't just hope she changed her mind.

It was time to act.

Three days had passed and Esperanza still had not returned. Nor had Peter, which was just as well.

Diego had been right to remind her that she could not forget what she was. Or what Peter was, no matter how tempting his kiss had been.

She hadn't seen his car in days. He hadn't called.

Which was how it should be—a clean, painless break. Only she missed their early morning cup of coffee—and that kiss.

Just as she was chastising herself for thinking about him again she saw his car, parked a few doors down from the shelter. Joy welled up in her, and she quickened her pace. She'd just walk over and say hello. Surely a friendly greeting wouldn't be enough to have her forgetting why they couldn't be together.

Keeping her gaze trained on his car, she failed to see the van coming down the block until it stopped next to her. Two men jumped out. With her vampire powers, two men presented little challenge. Except one of them pulled out an odd-looking gun and fired it.

Pain seared through her, jolting her with the blast coming from the barbs that penetrated her skin. She ripped them away to defend herself when Peter joined the fray.

He was in the midst of pulling his weapon just as the second man let loose with another odd-looking gun. Peter's body jerked backward as the barbs connected and power leaped through his body.

She couldn't delay. She transformed immediately, lashing out first at the wires connected to Peter and after, at their attackers.

One of the men raised a stick toward her, but never got to use it. She grabbed his arm and swung him into the man assaulting Peter. They went down in a heap on the sidewalk. Afraid to let up for even a moment, lest they attack with some other weapon, she brought her foot down on his arm and heard a satisfying snap, followed by his howl of pain. Peter's assailant, seeing that she hadn't been put down by their weapons, was already scrambling away. She grabbed him by the scruff of his neck and drove him headlong into the side of the van.

With both men immobile, she morphed back to her human state and raced to Peter's side. He was dazed from the weapon's blast so she picked him up and dragged him to the steps of the shelter.

Someone must have heard the commotion. The door flew open to reveal Sofia and a few other women from the shelter. "Should I call the police?" Sofia asked.

"No." If these men were the ones who had taken Samantha's friends, the last thing she needed was to have the police involved. "Help me get Peter to my room. Lock up the shelter."

As she and Sofia helped Peter, he tried to make his legs move but his actions were disjointed and uncoordinated. From behind her, she heard the locks on the door slip into place and the whispered comments of the other women as they debated her instructions.

When her gaze collided with Sofia's she realized the other woman also doubted her judgment but would not challenge it. "Trust me," was all she said, and Sofia nodded.

Peter was a heavy burden, almost entirely dead weight. It took all of their strength to get him to her room at the back of the first floor and gently onto the bed.

Sofia examined him, hands on her hips. "What did they use? He went down like a rock."

"Some kind of stun gun." She removed his shoes, and then with Sofia's help, took off his suit jacket, revealing the gun he hadn't been able to draw. To be on the safe side, they removed the gun and holster and she placed them in the drawer of her nightstand. "Would you get me a bowl with some ice water and a towel?"

Leslie, one of the other women in the shelter, stood by the door anxiously watching Samantha remove Peter's tie. "They're gone. But we got the license plate number," she said.

Samantha took the note as Sofia left to get the water. "I'll make sure the detective gets this as soon as he's able to make sense of it."

Leslie laid a hand on her arm. "Are you in some kind of trouble?"

Samantha met her gaze and then looked beyond her, to the other two women gathered in the hallway. This would be traumatic for them, having suffered through varied attacks in their lives. She was just thankful the children weren't awake to witness it as well.

"No, I'm not."

To a woman, they all looked away, as if they knew it was a lie, but were afraid to say more. Except for Sofia, who as she returned to the room said, "If you're in trouble, you can count on us, you know. You're not alone anymore."

Sofia's words brought untold comfort. She gave each of the other women a hug. "Go get some rest. I'll take care of the detective."

Sofia laid the small ceramic bowl with the ice water on the nightstand and stood looking down at Peter. "I don't trust cops, you know. But this guy…I think you can trust him, Samantha." She looked over her shoulder and repeated her earlier comment. "You're not alone. You've got us and you've got him, even though you might not want him."

The problem was that she did want him. But having him was fraught with too many complications.

After she urged Sofia out the door, Samantha dampened the towel and brought it to Peter's face, trying to rouse him. Over and over again, she passed it over his forehead and across his cheeks. Little by little, he regained his sensibilities.

"What happened?" He brought a hand to his forehead, as if to steady himself, and tried to rise.

Samantha placed her hand in the middle of his chest and pushed him back onto the bed. "Someone tried to grab me and you stopped them." She couldn't have him thinking she had somehow disarmed and escaped two men on her own. That would create too much suspicion.

Peter lay back against the pillows. "What did they hit me with? A Mack truck?"

"A stun gun." She moved her hand to his side, where she had seen the gun's barbs strike home. He winced and pulled his shirt out of his pants to reveal two nasty-looking marks.

"Shit. I have to call this in." He once again made to rise, but she easily restrained him.

"You're weak and you need to rest. The guys are long

gone, but we got the license plate number for you. When you're better," she added and was surprised when he grinned and flopped back onto the pillows.

"I won't argue with you 'cause I feel like shit and 'cause I like it when you get all empowered."

His comment dragged a smile to her face, despite the severity of what had just happened. "Get some rest. I'll be right back." She needed to call Diego and warn him.

Diego was upset, understandably so. "Someone knows where our lairs are. Now we are no longer safe even there."

"Watch yourself tonight, Diego. We'll talk in the morning about what to do next." She looked back toward the closed door to her room, wondering how she would explain it all to Peter.

There was a pause on the other end of the phone line before Diego said, "He's still there, isn't he?"

"Yes."

"In your room. In your bed. That is like playing with a loaded gun, *amiga.*"

Closing her eyes, she rubbed at her forehead. "I know what I'm doing, Diego."

"I hope so," he said and hung up.

She returned to her bedroom. Peter was still there. In her room. In her bed. No man had ever been in that bed before. But in her heart, she knew Peter wasn't just any man.

He was kind and gentle. Honorable. Incredibly handsome.

Her awareness of the last surprised her. She had her share of handsome men in her life. Ricardo. Diego. Even Blake. Stunning men who turned heads wherever they went.

But not one of them moved her like Peter did. Not one of them made her want to forget that she had sworn off men because of the pain they caused. Especially this one, whose every day was filled with the kind of violence she didn't want in her life. Who, like her, was capable of savagery—perhaps even against her, if he saw her demon emerge. He was definitely not the man she needed in her undead life.

Moving back to the bed, she watched him sleep. Admired the straight line of his nose, the perfect squareness of his jaw, the just right cleft in his chin. She admired those lips that knew how to kiss so well and the tanned skin and shaggy thick head of sun-streaked hair that screamed of beach and surf, of days spent in the sun. In the light.

His life was in the light. He deserved what human life could offer him. She'd seen the gentle way he played with the children, his patience as he explained a homework problem. She'd seen his kindness as he helped the women in the shelter with one thing or another. And she'd seen his bravery as he'd come to her rescue.

Would he have come to her rescue if he knew she was a vampire? No matter how much temptation called to her, she could never be the woman he wanted. She could never walk in the light with him or give him the children he deserved to have. She was a creature of the dark. It was better she stay that way.

But then he opened his eyes and gave her a sleepy smile. "You're not going to stand there all night, are you? Especially when I have the rest of this big bed all empty beside me."

To lie beside him, like a normal woman. To imagine the possibilities of what might have been.

The temptation was just too much to resist.

Chapter 13

She slipped into bed beside him, still fully dressed. She didn't dare change for fear that Peter might misinterpret her actions. And she needed the extra warmth, a chill had settled into her. A vampire reaction to the trauma of the stun gun and the loss of energy from transforming and dealing with her two would-be abductors.

She should have fed while he was still out of it, rather than watching him like a foolish schoolgirl staring at a pop idol. But she hadn't. So she had some trepidation as she tucked herself next to him. She laid her hand on his chest, and he covered it with his own.

"You're cold."

"It was a little chilly out there," she lied, something which she had been doing all night long.

"Yeah." He rubbed her hand as if to warm it. She sensed

the change in his body. The slight uneasiness before he turned so he could face her.

"Are you in some kind of trouble?"

She met his gaze. His hazel-green eyes were trained on her face, intense in their perusal. She couldn't keep lying to him. But she also couldn't tell him the truth. "Even if I was, it's not the kind of trouble you can help me with, Peter."

He traced the edges of her lips with his thumb. "Why not?"

She opened her mouth to speak and tasted the saltiness of his skin. Suddenly she didn't want to talk anymore. Suddenly all she wanted was to reexperience the wonder of his kiss. "Please, Peter. Let's not talk about this."

Reluctantly he said, "Okay. So what do you want to talk about?"

She smiled and brushed a shaggy lock of sunbleached hair away from his face. Then she shifted her hand down, cupped his jaw where the soft bristle of his evening beard was just emerging. Then lower still, to his wonderful lips, which still bore a sleepy little boy grin. "I don't want to talk."

Peter groaned and his body jumped to almost painful life.

He'd wanted more of what he'd found in their interlude of a few days ago, but then she'd turned him away. Honestly, her reaction had pissed him off. But only a little. He'd sensed that she was conflicted about her feelings for him. He'd hoped to get a second chance with her. And now this.

He urged her closer with one hand, while tunneling his other into the thick mass of her wavy black hair.

She was so beautiful. He closed the last distance between them, barely brushing his lips against hers, and experiencing another jolt of surprise, in her body and his, at just how right it was. He'd never thought he could respond like this again after what had happened with his wife. Somehow being with Samantha brought deep pleasure and relief.

Maybe, just maybe, there could be more. He deepened his kiss, opening his mouth against hers to explore the textures and taste of her lips, savoring her tentative response which slowly grew bolder and more intoxicating. Her tongue danced against his. Over and over they kissed, until they were gripping one another tightly.

Until it wasn't enough.

He was the first to take the next step, easing his hand beneath her sweater to release the clasp on her bra.

She stiffened and he stopped, feeling the trembling of her body. "Are you okay?" He called himself a fool for not remembering that in Samantha's life, sex hadn't necessarily been a good thing.

"It's just… It's been a long time," she said and watched as the truth of her words registered with him. It had been a way, way long time, she thought. Much longer than he could imagine.

"It's been a long time for me as well. Do you want to stop?"

Ever the hero. She'd never had a hero in her bed before. Never a protector. Never someone who actually cared a whit about what she was feeling. Yet her wanting was tinged with fear. How would she react to his touch? Would the vampire within rise up, out of control as passion grew?

Already the heat of the beast inside her warmed her skin. She loved the taste of him, in ways that were not necessarily good. But she didn't want him to stop. Maybe that was selfish, but she wanted to know what it was like to be loved with gentleness and care.

"No. I don't want to stop."

Slowly, as if knowing her acquiescence was a troubled

one, he barely brushed his thumb across her nipple, restraining himself.

"That feels good." She reached for the buttons on his shirt, undoing them so she could slip her hand to the warm skin beneath.

Peter checked his need, detecting her hesitation, the shakiness of her hand as she laid it on his chest. He needed to go slowly with her. Make sure she knew he wasn't like the other men in her life.

With that in mind, his movements were patient. He explored her breast, holding it in his hand while bringing her nipple to a hard peak with his thumb. Her skin was satiny and smooth. A little warmer now, but still cold.

He shifted closer to heat her body with his and his hips butted against hers. She stiffened at the feel of his erection and gazed up at him with a mixture of longing and concern.

"We stop whenever you want. We do whatever you want to do."

Samantha didn't want to stop. Not just yet. Although the beast within was awakening along with her desire, she could still control it. And as long as she could, she wanted to savor being with this caring and loving man. Maybe she could even hold off the beast long enough to make love with him.

"I'm still cold, can you warm me up?" She reached for the hem of her sweater even before he did, but when she tossed it aside, she suddenly felt awkward. Exposed. She covered herself with her arms.

Peter wrapped his arms around her and pulled her tight to him. He moved his hands against her back in a soothing gesture. "Don't be afraid of me. I would never hurt you."

How she yearned to believe that. Yet she had no doubt that if he knew what she really was, he wouldn't hesitate to hurt her. As a cop, he was forced into decisions like that all the time. Driving those disturbing thoughts away, she snuggled against him and relished the heat of his body, the tenderness of his movements.

But the animal in her refused to stay still. It memorized the scent of his skin, strained to hear the *lub-dub* of his heart and the singing of the blood rushing through his veins. The beast began to awaken and her body warmed.

"That's better," he said, obviously noting the change in the temperature of her skin.

"Yes. Thank you." She drew away from him, giving him an unobstructed view of her breasts.

His gaze dipped down, much as she had expected it would. He was a man after all. He caressed her arm before slowly moving his hand to just above the swell of her right breast. He paused to trace the gentle rise with his fingers.

"I love the feel of your skin. The color of it, like coffee ice cream."

His words brought a smile to her lips. "Ice cream, Detective? You do have a sweet tooth, don't you?"

"Hmm." He slowly cupped her breast. Then he surprised her by taking the peaked tip of her nipple between his thumb and forefinger.

It dragged a shocked gasp from her. "Can I taste?" he asked. "See if it's as delicious as it looks?"

She could only nod, then he bent his head, brushed his lips against the hard peak. His movements were tender as he sampled her.

She closed her eyes against the sight and feel of him. The emotions were so intense her body was shaking with both fear and passion.

Gently he kissed her nipple, alternating his fingers and

mouth until she moaned and held his head to her. It was only then that he relented and wrapped his lips around the hard tip. Heat raced along her nerve endings and between her legs. She grew damp with wanting him, with the need for his sensitive and tender loving.

She opened her eyes, mesmerized, the tug of his kiss creating a sympathetic pull inside. It was so strong, she had to part her legs and, in tune with her, he lowered his hand to her buttocks and drew her leg over his.

He slipped his thigh between hers, until it was tucked against her center. The pressure assuaged her need…but just a little. Desire was growing almost faster than she could control it.

Peter was so hard, it was painful, but he kept his desire in check, knowing how fragile this was between them, how delicate her emotions were. Dragging himself from the sweetness of her breast, he met her lips, wanting her to be with him as they moved toward making love.

Her opened mouth sent a shock wave roiling through him. It hadn't been his imagination the other day. Their kiss had been that wonderful. It was as amazing tonight. Repeatedly he savored the shape and feel of her mouth with his lips. Tasting the freshness of her breath and relishing the slide of her tongue as the kiss grew more intense.

He pressed his thigh to her center, and, through the fabric of his pants, the heat and damp of her arousal called to him. All across her body, the chill from earlier was gone, replaced by a delicious heat.

He moved his hand down, taking his time as he skimmed along her smooth skin and slender torso. Past her ribs to her waist, where he shifted inward and found the tempting indentation of her navel. He slipped his thumb against the perfect hollow and she shivered.

"Sshh," he whispered against her lips. "We'll take it slow, Samantha."

"Peter." He almost came at the needy sound of his name on her lips. He wanted to hear her cry it out as they moved together.

His erection butted against her hips, reminding Samantha of where this would lead—if she could control the beast that was battling to emerge.

She laid her head beside his, met his lips in another kiss. Between her legs, there was an intense ache and she ground down onto his thigh to relieve the yearning.

Heat built within her as the smells of their arousal scented the air. When he lowered his head to her breast once more and gently teethed her nipple, she cried out in pleasure. But that tender bite inflamed the beast.

Samantha closed her eyes and struggled against it, bringing her head tight against the fresh clean smell of Peter's hair, reminding herself of sunlight and his humanity.

She had almost restored control, when he slipped free the fastening on her jeans and found the core of her with his fingers.

The feel of him sent her over the edge and released the demon.

Chapter 14

Her shove was so forceful Peter had to grab the edge of the mattress to keep from going over the side. Before he knew what was happening, she raced past him and into the bathroom. The door slammed shut with a resounding thud.

He lay on the bed, his breathing heavy with passion. He took but a moment for a deep breath and then walked to the door of the bathroom. "Samantha. Are you okay?"

"I'm sorry, Peter," she said. "So sorry." The rough sound of her voice carried through the door.

"It's okay, Samantha. I understand," He wished she would open the door and let him comfort her.

"You can't possibly understand. Go away, Peter."

It was useless to argue with her right now. Her emotions were too conflicted and too fragile. So instead, he put on his shirt and sat in a comfortable-looking rocker in the far corner of the room.

He would wait for her.

She lay curled into a ball at the foot of the door. With her ear pressed to the wood, she heard his movements and then nothing.

The wait allowed her to regain control. She was back to being human, but she needed to feed. Tonight's physical and emotional roller coaster ride had drained her. Making sure the door was still locked, she moved to the large vanity. From the small refrigerator tucked within, she extracted not one, but two blood bags.

She quickly drained both of them, carefully wrapped them in a garbage bag for disposal, and rinsed her mouth clean. She peered into the vacant mirror. It had been so long since she'd seen her reflection, she wondered how she appeared to humans. What about her had caught Peter's interest?

Peter. If tonight had taught her one thing it was that she couldn't control herself enough to be with him.

Shaking her head, she slipped out of her jeans and tossed them into the corner by the tub. At the door, she grabbed her terry cloth robe from the hook and eased it on. Belting it tightly, she went back into her bedroom, her mind and gaze focused on the empty bed. She laid her hand on the indentation where he'd rested. It was still warm. Or maybe she was just imagining that it was.

"I'm still here."

She jumped at the sound of his voice and whirled to find him sitting in her rocker. The question escaped her lips before she could stop it. "Why?"

"Why?" he repeated. He walked toward her, stopping about a foot away, as if aware she couldn't handle anything more. "I know you've had a rough life. That you may have issues."

"You can't even imagine."

"I don't want to imagine. I want you to tell me. When you're ready. I want you to trust me enough to tell me what happened tonight."

He cupped her cheek once again and despite her misgivings, she leaned into the tenderness of that simple caress, and found herself back in his arms, gripping him tightly.

"I'm sorry, Peter. I'm not sure I'll ever be ready."

His hold on her tightened and his tone was hard as he said, "Maybe we rushed things, but in time—"

She silenced him with a harsh laugh and pulled away. Time? She had all the time in the world and then some. And even with all that time, it wouldn't be enough to forget all the hurt she'd suffered. This whole human-vampire thing was impossible no matter how much time she was willing to devote. "You can't possibly understand, Peter."

"Understand what? That you were abused? That your life so far has sucked?"

His voice was rough with emotion and she saw the pain in his gaze. He'd been hurt, too. "I'm sorry if you've suffered also, but that doesn't change this—"

"This? What's this?"

"This being what I am. What you are." She motioned to both of them with her hand.

"What are you?" he asked, bending toward her to search her face.

"Different."

He straightened and dragged a hand through the shaggy locks of his hair in exasperation. "Different," he repeated. "Is that why those two men were after you tonight. Because you're different?"

They were treading on dangerous ground. "Just leave it alone, Peter." She turned away from him, but he grabbed her arm and pressured her to face him once more.

"You don't have to deal with this alone anymore, Samantha. You can't. Too many people rely on you. Too many people care for you."

Emotion rose up sharply within her. Raw and demanding. She'd been alone for so long and she'd handled it. She'd never thought that having others—especially human others—in her life would complicate it so. They were fragile and could be hurt if those men came back. And then there were her vampire friends, disappearing too regularly. Not as fragile and yet still in need of protection.

She looked up at Peter. Of all the things she knew about him, she was most certain of two—Peter was both a hero and a protector. Danger had come to the front steps of her home and he'd helped her vanquish it. Maybe it was time to trust him, before things got any worse.

"Three of my friends are missing."

He seemed surprised that she had confided in him, but quickly schooled that emotion. "Why haven't you called the police?"

She shrugged and wrapped her arms around herself, contemplating how to explain and how to lie. "We're different, Peter. We live on the edge—"

"Which means you're not the kind of people the police usually help? I'm here. I'm willing to help." He held his hands out, not only to stress his point, it seemed to her, but to invite her into his arms. But she couldn't place herself in his hands. Not just yet.

"We frequent The Blood Bank." She sat on the edge of the bed.

Peter crouched in front of her, smack in the middle of her line of sight, where it was impossible not to see him. Or for him not to see her, she realized.

"I had to question someone at that bar once. It's a rough place and barely legal. Why do you—"

"Does it matter why we go there? We do."

"Because you're…different. And now three of you—"

"Are missing," she finished for him.

He reached into his suit jacket and withdrew his notepad. As he did so, she noticed that he'd slipped his holster back on. His gun, shiny, black and deadly, was tucked beneath his arm, ready for use.

He must have sensed where her attention had been drawn. "It's part of what I do."

"I know." Just as she knew that he'd killed with it recently. Would he use it against her one day? Or against one of her friends? Maybe she should rethink not only his offer to help, but any kind of involvement with him. "This isn't a good idea."

Myriad emotions flashed across her face and Peter was hard-pressed to understand her fear. Until it occurred to him that perhaps, in her life, no one had helped her before. That she was distrustful of the systems that had failed her. Which for some reason made him think of his FBI agent friend Diana Reyes.

They'd worked together on two different cases now and in both instances, he'd sensed there was something not quite normal with Diana's lover, Ryder, and their friends. Diana had never confided in him, but when she'd asked Peter for help during her last case, he hadn't been reluctant to do what she'd asked. Just as he knew that if he called, Diana would come without hesitation. Maybe it was time to call in his marker.

"I have a friend. I think she could help us because… There's something different about her as well."

Samantha looked puzzled. "Why would she help you? Help us?"

"She's a straight-up kind of person and I helped her out a little while ago."

Once again, he detected a mix of emotions, concern followed by acceptance. "I guess I don't have much choice, do I? Because I suspect you won't leave me alone until I cave, right?"

He smiled. "What makes you think I'll leave you alone now that you have caved?"

She shook her head and smiled in response. "I don't know what to say, Peter. How to thank you."

He took hold of her hand and rose, bringing her up with him. "I'm just doing what's right, Samantha."

"Right. What's right," she repeated sadly. Peter wanted to comfort her, but found that he couldn't. He was confused himself about what he was getting into. After all, she'd made it clear she might not ever be ready for a relationship and he understood her feelings only too well. He still didn't know if he was ready for one himself. Especially given the secrets Samantha refused to share and the way his last serious relationship had ended.

With that thought, he promised he'd make some calls and be back soon. Samantha smiled at that, and he told himself not to read too much into it. Nor in the embrace they shared at the door.

Because if he did, he might only be setting himself up for a big disappointment.

Chapter 15

Edward had learned from his mistakes. Too many bodies led to too many questions. As angry as he was with his minions for failing to grab his next specimen, he had to keep them around for another try. But not right away. That would only arouse too much suspicion, especially if as his assistants said, Samantha Turner had a cop hanging around.

Edward had done a little research but had unearthed nothing on Ms. Turner, except one article about the shooting in front of her shelter. That would explain the police officer. But two of the suspects had been killed and the third seemed to have flown. Which meant that police surveillance was likely to stop soon.

He could wait another few days. He still had the other two vamps to play with.

Too bad about the third, rather plain one. But then again, she'd lacked the spirit of his earlier captives. Lacked their fire.

He wondered if that was why she'd succumbed so easily despite her age.

No matter. His goons had tossed her body onto a small secluded patch of meadow just behind the building. The punk vamp—Blake—had said the sun would take care of her remains and he had been right. With just a few early morning hours of sunlight, Esperanza's body had shriveled as the sun emptied her life's fluids. By noon, she'd barely been more than skin over skeleton.

As Edward had watched the decomposition, it occurred to him just what he could use her for. His assistants brought her body back inside rather than letting the process continue until she was just a pile of dust.

It was amazing really. Such strong creatures in the night, but so frail during the day.

That was the mistake he had made with Ms. Turner. He should never have sent his men after her at night, when she was strongest. They needed to attack during the day when she'd be weaker. When she'd be alone in the shelter.

But not now when the detective might be lingering. The female vampire had revealed the identity of another of her friends. He would not expect someone to be after him, Edward thought, turning his attention to the screen, where his two captives were visible from the camera mounted in the far corner of their cage. The female cradled her wounded mate, rocked him in her arms like a mother might a child.

The young punk vamp had been weak after today's trials and bloodletting. Maybe too weak. It might be wise to wait another few days before experimenting with him again. Or with the female. She was the more delicate of the two.

Tapping his finger against his lips, he considered the delays in his plans. He needed another transfusion, but he couldn't risk losing either of these subjects before seizing another, stronger one.

Ms. Turner or her friend Diego might eventually help him solve the puzzle of immortality, but he had to catch them first. Until then he needed to keep these two alive and relatively well. He really should give them a bag or two of blood. Maybe after he watched them feed off one another and share a vampire's kind of love—sex and blood mixed into a sensual and violent dance.

Once the vampire's blood in his veins cured him, would he feel the fires of his youth once more? He longed for the yearnings and drive his old, sick body could no longer support.

Ay, youth, he thought after the platinum-haired Blake plunged into Meghan while she sank her teeth into his neck. It was truly wasted on the young.

Peter knew her number by heart.

"Special Agent Reyes," she answered and he teased her as he always did. "Very Special Agent Reyes."

"Peter." There was genuine affection in her tone. "How are you?"

"It's been a rough couple of weeks." He explained to her about the drive-by shooting case and all that had happened, including his killing two of the suspects.

"I'm sorry. I know that must have been hard for you."

"So many dead, Diana. And I still can't understand why."

"I wish I had an answer, but I don't. I also know that isn't the only reason you're calling," she said and in the background, he heard someone talking. Her voice was muffled as she said, "I need to take this call." She had probably covered the mouthpiece with her hand.

When she came back on, she said, "I'm sorry. It's a zoo around here."

"Let me not keep you," he said, reconsidering his earlier decision to ask for her help given how busy she sounded.

"Peter, this is me, remember. If you need something, I'm here."

He breathed a sigh of relief and blurted out, "That's good, because I think I need your help." Explaining about Samantha, he finished by saying, "Whatever we do, it needs to be private, Diana."

"It goes no further than me, and maybe Ryder. I think he knows about The Blood Bank. He may be able to help us."

Peter sensed his friend knew just how important this case was to him. "Can the two of you come over tonight? Meet Samantha and hear what she has to say?"

"We'll be there."

Peter gave her the address for the shelter.

It was late. Samantha had asked that Peter arrange the meeting at a time when the women and children were in bed and asleep. She didn't want them to know about her problem.

"Thanks for coming at such an odd hour," he said and motioned for Ryder and Diana to make themselves comfortable on the couch. "Samantha is downstairs making some coffee. She'll be up in a second."

"You didn't say what was up on the phone." Diana shot an uneasy glance between him and Ryder.

Ryder was clearly jealous of Peter, thinking Peter might make a play for Diana. In the past, he might have. Only now, his interests lay elsewhere.

And Ryder was aware of Peter's assistance in saving Ryder's friend, Melissa Danvers, nearly a year ago when she'd been kidnapped.

Peter had no doubt that Diana would help Samantha. As

for Ryder…Peter suspected he was a man of honor who recognized when a debt was owed. Peter had just called in that debt.

"Samantha has some friends who are missing," he said. "The last place all of them were seen was at The Blood Bank."

"Some patrons at The Lair mentioned that bar to me, so I went for a visit. A bad place to be," Ryder interjected.

Peter nodded. "I agree, only that doesn't change what's happened. Any suggestions?"

Diana leaned forward. "Let's hear what Samantha has to say, first. Maybe then we can decide what to do."

Footsteps sounded on the wooden floor of the hall as Samantha stepped into the room. The china she carried rattled and she dropped the tray she was carrying. There was a muffled crash as it hit the rug, followed by an angry rumbling sound, like that of a large jungle cat.

Peter whirled to see what had made the sound and froze in his place, unable to believe what he was seeing.

Ryder had jumped to his feet, his hands clenched into fists by his side. His eyes glowed with an unnaturally bright light and before Peter's eyes, long fangs erupted from Ryder's mouth. Peter drew his weapon and trained it on the thing that Ryder had become. Diana stepped in the way of his shot.

She held Ryder back when he would have launched himself across the room. "Ryder, stop. What are you doing?"

Samantha was suddenly at Peter's back. He turned to find her transforming. Mutating into something…

Her marvelous blue eyes turned cold and a bright otherworldly light bled into her irises. From beneath the edge of her top lip, her incisors elongated, inching downward until the now lethal-looking fangs nearly reached midchin. A strange aura of power surrounded her.

"Holy shit." He raised his gun, placed it point-blank in the middle of her chest.

"You told me once that you would never hurt me. Would you do it now, Peter?" she asked, her voice low, with a rumbly edge. She stepped toward him, and it took all his strength to keep his weapon trained on her as he battled his confused emotions about the creature she'd become.

"Stop, Samantha." He would shoot her before he let her take any action against his friends.

"You *would* shoot me, wouldn't you? You have little fear of violence, but then again, neither do Ryder and I." She raised her hand to cup his cheek, but he took a step back, fear churning in his stomach.

"What are you?" But he already knew the answer. An impossible answer. One out of comic books and horror movies. Not one out of real life.

"She's a vampire, Peter. She's the one who made me what I am," Ryder said with deadly calm.

Chapter 16

1863, a Civil War battlefield

Samantha walked among the bodies, her long skirt trailing through blood and gore. So much violence and destruction. So much loss of precious life.

There were more dead here than wounded on the battlefield. And those that were wounded would soon be gone, drained of life by the band of vampires lurking in the night, seeking out such easy prey. Her stomach turned at the thought that she, too, would feed soon. The smell of the blood had started the change over which she had little control. She was still too young a vampire to have much command over where and when she transformed.

Disgusted with her need, she walked to the farthest edge of the battlefield, near a copse of trees where some combatants had sought shelter from the barrage of gunfire.

The light of the full moon was strong tonight, exposing the inhumanity of the fight. Near the woods, there were mostly gray uniforms, stained with blood.

Samantha was nearly dizzy from need. It had been a week since she'd fed. She only fed when she had to and even then, asked herself why she did so. Why did she cling so futilely to the twisted life she'd been given? Why didn't she just end her miserable existence?

Some spark of hope remained in her. Some spark of humanity that kept her from killing like the others.

That hope, that humanity was why she stood at the edge of the moonlit killing field, searching out someone newly dead. Fresh blood was always the most powerful. The more powerful it was, the longer she could wait to feed again.

She spotted one young soldier, barely feet away. Even with the distance between them, she heard the butterfly beat of his heart. She walked over, knelt beside him. He was so young, he hardly had a beard. And here he was, dying all alone.

Tears came to her eyes. She had died much the same way, but she wouldn't let that happen to him. She held his hand tightly. With the last of his strength, the young soldier grabbed her weakly, as if trying to cling to life.

She comforted him as best she could, speaking to him gently until that fluttery beat stopped and his dark brown eyes glazed over in death. Tenderly she cradled him, willing his soul peace in the afterlife. Asking forgiveness for what she would do next.

Easing open the collar on the rough wool jacket of his uniform, she lowered her head.

Screams of men dying pierced the night. Not the cries of wounded men. No, these were the shouts of the able-bodied. Shots followed as they tried to defend themselves against their attackers.

Samantha dropped the young soldier and raced toward the struggle, disbelieving that the other vampires would be so bold as to attack a large group of armed soldiers. She dodged trees, branches and brush whipping against her as she sped through the woods. Scrambling one way and then another, over tangled roots and fallen logs, in her haste to reach the battle. One between human and vampire.

As she emerged from the far edge of the woods, she realized why the vampires had been so bold. This was no large group of soldiers. Just a small contingent of medics and doctors tending to the wounded. The larger battalion must have moved on, leaving the medical unit behind.

The shots were fewer now as most of the men had been overtaken by the members of her group. She watched as they fed on one healthy man or another. From within the tent, the shadows on the canvas walls played out a gruesome scene. Still disbelieving they could be so callous, she raced to the entry of the tent and stopped dead at the sight greeting her. Vampires moved from one wounded man to another, feeding freely on those too weak to defend themselves. Pitiful moans and pleas, along with the glee of the vampires, filled the tent.

Samantha couldn't watch anymore.

She fled outside, where things were not much better. The stronger vampires, who took delight not just in feeding, but in the fight of their prey, were grappling with the able-bodied soldiers. Their struggles were a grim ballet in the bright moonlight. Here, as on the battlefield, the smell of blood was strong. The vampires' attacks spilled fresh wetness onto the men's uniforms and onto the ground. A wasted feast, but her group was not interested in creating others to add to their number. That would make for more competition in feeding, so after they had nearly drained their victims, they left them to die rather than turning them.

Samantha approached one fallen man, hunger driving her. But then she heard someone cry out. There was something familiar about the voice. Another cry came and she searched out its source.

Ten or more feet away, the moonlight played against the grotesque silhouette of four of her group, viciously dining on one poor man. Latched on to his arms and legs, they were tearing into him like a wild pack of hyenas. As he pleaded, they tugged and shook him. He turned his face up to the moonlight and cried out for assistance, his pleas weaker than from the moment before.

Samantha froze as his face was revealed to her. Dr. Ryder Latimer. One of the few men who had been kind to her in her other life.

"No." Running toward him, she shouted and fully transformed. By the time she reached the gruesome scene, her shouts had become warning growls. The intensity of her anger ripped her compatriots from their feast. Although they were not much older than she was and were her equals strength-wise, the ferocity of her snarling warnings drove them away from their feast.

Dr. Latimer dropped to the ground limply.

Samantha stopped short and took note of his wounds. Dark, almost black blood stained each leg. A neat round hole in the middle of his abdomen. She'd seen enough of those during this horrible conflict to know he had been shot. Probably a stray bullet from someone trying to defend themselves. Blood seeped from wounds on his arms, but the greatest damage was on his neck, where one of the vampires had nearly torn his throat open.

She dropped to the ground beside him, quickly ripped some fabric from her underskirt, balled it and pressed it to his throat, trying to staunch the flow of blood. At her touch, he turned his head and his eyes widened in recognition.

"Samantha." There was a slight gurgle in his voice as blood washed into this windpipe.

"Dr. Latimer. Try to rest. You'll be fine," she said, although she wasn't sure. The fabric she had pressed to his wound was already drenched and when he coughed, fresh blood stained his lips. He was bleeding internally as well, maybe from the bullet wound.

The ground was cold beneath her legs and she wanted to protect him from it. He might be cold soon enough. Pain tore through her at the idea of him dead. He'd been too good to her. Too kind. This shouldn't be the way his life ended.

She slipped her arm beneath his back and cradled him tightly to her body. Only there was no warmth there. Nothing she could give to ease his suffering.

"Cold," he said, his voice barely a whisper.

She held him tighter, bent and kissed his forehead. "You'll be warm soon."

With surprising strength, he grabbed her arm. "Don't…want…to…die." After his words, he coughed and more blood stained his lips.

Tears came to her eyes and a sudden errant thought. "I can help you," she said and laid her hand on his uniform. Beneath her fingers beat his struggling heart. It grew more erratic and weaker by the second. His breath was shallow and barely stirred the air as he said, "Help…me."

Taking a deep breath, she gave in to the change she'd been battling since she'd first smelled his blood, rich against her nostrils. Warm against her hand as she tried to staunch its flow. Heat flared through every cell in her body and strength came with it. Incredible and inhuman strength.

She glanced around, seeking out the others in her group. They would stop her if they knew what she was about to do. Maybe even kill her after she'd done it. Only the eldest in this group were permitted to bestow the ultimate kiss. It had been one of those elders who'd sired her to replace the paramour he'd lost.

Easing her other arm beneath Ryder's legs, she effortlessly lifted him as the vamp within her assumed control. Quickly she moved with him to the edge of the woods, slipping within its leafy edges until she was hidden from view.

She laid Ryder on the ground. The edges of his collar were stained with the blood oozing from the ragged wound at his neck. She watched that blood and the shallow rise of his chest. He was dying, but he didn't want to die. He didn't deserve to die and she had promised to help him, much as he had helped her.

Bending, she brought her mouth to that wound, and mimicking what she had seen older vampires do, licked it.

The blood spiced her lips and her fangs elongated even more, but she fought the desire to sink her teeth into his neck. Instead, she gave lick after lick and watched as his skin slowly knitted closed. Pleased with her result, she slipped her hand over his chest, hopeful that her ministrations had helped, but there was still barely a beat there.

His gaze was almost as wide and unfocused as that of the young soldier she'd tended to earlier in the night. "Ryder." She grabbed hold of his hand.

No response greeted her.

Ripping open his jacket, she took note of the angry bullet wound and the blood that still escaped. As before, she bent and licked the wound, hoping the magic of her kiss would reach within and heal his internal wounds.

She fed a bit as she tried to heal him, but even after her ministrations he was still unresponsive. When she picked up her head, she noted the wound on his leg.

She'd thought it minor at first, but now realized one of her group had severely damaged Ryder's femoral artery. His pant leg was drenched in blood. She might not be able to fix the wound in time to save him.

His face was pale. His eyes almost glazed over.

"No." She laid her hand on his chest. It was still warm, but growing colder. Beneath her hand, there was hardly a beat. Only a faint fluttering. Despite all her efforts, he'd be dead soon. Unless…

She couldn't let him die.

Bending, she cradled him in her arms once again. He was silent this time. She brought him up in her arms until the side of his neck was exposed. The scars were still there from the earlier attack, but fading quickly. Had he lived, he would have borne no scars from this encounter. But he wouldn't live tonight. At least not as a human.

He'd be reborn.

Samantha sank her fangs into his neck and fed until she sensed his heart clinging to the last beats of life. It took all of her strength not to keep feeding until no life remained and his soul passed onto another plane.

Pulling away from him, she used her fangs to slice open the wrist on her free hand and brought the wound to his lips. At first there was no response, but then his mouth moved. He seemed to be pulling away, as if fighting her offering, but she held his head close and forced him to feed.

Soon he latched on to the wound, licking and sucking until some strength had returned. He ripped his head away then and with anguished eyes asked, "Why?"

Chapter 17

"Why?" Ryder asked again, much as he had more than a century earlier.

"Because you'd been kind to me. I couldn't let you die." She moved toward him, even as Peter jabbed the middle of her chest with his gun.

As she met Peter's gaze, something stirred within her. Something that drove home all that she had lost. She saw nothing but horror and disgust in Peter's eyes. His response drained her of the defensive anger that had erupted when Ryder had morphed, ready to attack.

Returning to her human form, she said to Peter, "Shoot me if you want. Not that it will do much good."

Although he kept his gun trained on her, she sensed his weakness. His indecision. She gripped the barrel of the pistol and eased it from his grasp. "I didn't think you could."

"But I can." Ryder again moved toward her, but once again, Ryder's companion blocked his way.

Samantha pleaded her case once more. "You would have died that night from the wounds the other vampires inflicted on you."

"I almost died after, from the change that made me like you. Made me an animal." He pushed toward her once more, but this time the woman with Ryder drew her own weapon and aimed it in his direction.

"I know this won't kill you, Ryder. But it will surely slow you down. Please don't make me use it."

"Darlin'," he said, and she lowered her gun. "She's the one who made me this way."

Samantha couldn't see the other woman's face and so it was difficult to know what she was thinking. She could tell what Peter was still thinking, however. Disgust. Betrayal. Anger. Hurt. The emotions had been painted on his face by her actions.

"I'm sorry." She reached out to him, but he stepped away from her.

At her words, the woman standing in front of Ryder turned. Young. Beautiful. Human. Clearly involved with the angry vampire standing behind her. She surprised Samantha by holstering her gun and walking over to her. "Is it true? Are you the one who sired him?"

Samantha wouldn't deny it. She couldn't. "I'm the one."

"Then I want to thank you," she said and held out her hand.

Shocked, Samantha nevertheless shook the woman's hand. "I only wanted to help."

"Like you helped those kids the night of the drive-by shooting?" Peter asked as he retrieved his gun.

"I got three of them out of the way. It was all I could do."

"And now you want our help?" Diana asked. She bent and began to pick up the shattered pieces of china.

The two women cleaned up what they could. They rose together, Samantha holding the tray and Diana looking at the two men who stood feet apart, warily glancing at one another. She addressed Ryder first. "Will you help?"

Ryder's answer came quickly. "No." With that, he walked to the door and left the shelter.

Diana let out a harsh sigh and turned her attention to Peter. "And you? Will you help?"

Peter glanced from Diana to Samantha, and then back to Diana. "I need to speak to you, Diana. In private."

He gave Samantha a harsh glare and she responded immediately, rushing from the room with a feeble, "I'll put on a fresh pot of coffee."

He watched her go, as did Diana. When Samantha was gone Diana immediately lambasted him. "Why don't you just pistol-whip her and get it over with? It might hurt her less."

"Hurt her less?" He advanced on his friend angrily. "She lied to me. Christ, I almost—" He bit back what he was about to say, realizing it would reveal too much.

"I wanted to hurt him when I found out. I barely kept from kicking his ass," Diana admitted.

"When did you find out?" Peter asked, still dumbfounded by all that had happened.

Diana walked over to the sofa and sat down. "During the Williams investigation. His keeper—"

"Keeper? What the hell's a keeper?"

"The person who helps vampires when they're weak or hurt. Who keeps them safe in their lairs when they rest."

"Them? You act as if they're human." Peter dragged a hand through his hair as it sank in once again that Samantha was not.

"Ryder may as well be. He stays in his human form when he can and tries to live during the daylight hours. Plus, he rarely feeds on other humans."

It took a moment for her last words to register. "Rarely? He's fed on you, hasn't he?"

"Peter, that doesn't really matter." She raised her hand to stress that maybe he was asking for too much information, but that didn't stop him.

"He's your lover and you've let him feed from you." His words were cold and condemning.

"You think I had a choice in falling in love with him? Or helping him when he needed me?"

Who cared for Samantha? Who watched over her and made sure she was well?

The answer immediately came to mind as he recalled who had come forth the night of the shooting. Ricardo, the *santero*. She'd been injured badly that night. The bloodied shirt had been proof of that. Had Samantha fed on the *santero* to heal herself? An unexpected pang of jealousy rose up in him, but he quickly tamped it down. He shouldn't be caring about her.

She wasn't human. Only…

In all the time he'd spent with her, her caring ways had called to him. Her ability to deal with things despite the suffering life had bestowed on her made him admire her strength of will and character. And her selfless desire to help others, her humanity, had impressed him. *Her humanity.* Once again, the vision of the demon rose up and destroyed all the good things he knew about her. Made him fear her enough that he would have pulled the trigger on her. After all, it wasn't like he was a man who didn't know how to kill. And maybe that was what scared him about tonight's discovery the most—that deep within, they were very similar creatures.

"Peter?"

He realized Diana had asked him another question he hadn't even heard.

"I'm sorry. My mind was elsewhere."

Diana nodded and inclined her head in the direction of the hallway. "On the lady downstairs."

Anger roared to life as Samantha's deception registered once again. "She's not a lady. She's…I can't believe it, Diana. It's just not possible."

"They're vampires, Peter. It was hard for me to conceive of it as well, but there's no denying their existence."

Peter dragged a hand through his hair and shook his head. "I trusted her."

"I know that you…cared for her. That her keeping the truth from you hurts, but would you have believed her if she had told you?"

Her question deflated some of his anger. "Probably not. But that doesn't change the fact that she's a demon."

"Look at all the killers we battle. They're all human. Like us, there are good and bad amongst vampires." As she said that, she covered his hand with hers. "Don't judge her too harshly, Peter. I'm sure her life hasn't been easy."

No, it hadn't been. He remembered the faint scars on her back. Scars her husband had placed there in addition to the ones on her heart. Had she voluntarily become a vampire or had she been taken against her will? Had she made vampires besides Ryder? There was a score of things he didn't know about her world and he wasn't sure he wanted to know.

"Peter? Will you help?" Diana asked again. She squeezed his hand as if to reassure him that she would understand no matter what he decided.

Only he didn't know what answer to give. Not yet. "I need

to speak to…" He hesitated, not sure he could call Samantha a lady, and yet unable to name her a vampire. He was still having trouble with the whole idea. After taking a deep swallow, he finished with, "Samantha and I need to discuss some things. Can you give me a few minutes?"

She nodded. "I'll wait here."

Samantha had made a pot of coffee. Its rich smell greeted him when he stepped into the kitchen.

She was sitting at a large oak table, her back to the door. Her arms were crossed, pillowing her head. Her position pulled the off-white sweater she wore upward, exposing the fine network of scars along her lower waist. At the tops of her shoulders, the scoop of her neckline revealed more of the same.

He wanted to reach for her to soothe her hurt, but he quickly shoved his hands into the pockets of his jeans.

She hadn't stirred since he'd entered the room, but she clearly knew he was there. She stared straight ahead as she said, "I thought you would have followed Ryder out the door."

Peter stood to the right of her, where he could see her face, but she didn't spare him a glance. "I needed some answers first."

She nodded and clasped her hands together tightly. "It's your right."

"Damn straight it's my right," he said angrily and leaned forward, gripping the top of the chair in front of him. "I thought we were starting something—"

"We were." She finally faced him. Her eyes glistened with unshed tears. He couldn't help being moved by the sight until he remembered what she was and how she had betrayed him.

"Save the waterworks. My ex-wife used the same tactic. I'm immune by now."

She inclined her head upward, but when she did so, the first tear escaped her. She swiped at it harshly, as if angry with herself for being unable to control it. "I'm not like your wife."

"Ex-wife," he corrected. "She was oh so solicitous. Like you. Beautiful. Like you. She betrayed me. Just like you betrayed me by lying about what you are."

"What was I supposed to do? 'Hi, I'm Samantha Turner, vampire.' Would you have believed me if I'd told you? And don't you realize I might have endangered you with the truth?"

He had no answers to her questions. Had she told him, he would have either thought her insane and backed away—no matter how beautiful she was—or tried to get more information. If he'd done the latter, maybe he would have been in danger, but by not telling him… "Why the charade of letting me get close?"

She'd lied to him from day one, Samantha thought, but she couldn't keep on lying now. What would be the sense? Her deepest darkest secret was already out in the open. "It wasn't a charade. If anything, I told myself time and time again that I shouldn't let you in."

Not that he'd given her much of a choice, always being there. Always watching out for her. Letting her know that he wasn't going to go away.

"I shouldn't have let you in," she repeated weakly.

"I didn't give you much choice, did I?"

Gazing up at him, she said, "No, you didn't. In my entire life, no man had ever looked at me like you did. Treated me with the kindness and honor you brought into my life."

"And so you paid me back for that by lying to me?"

Once more, she had no defense against his accusation. Except one. "I wanted to know what it was like to be loved," she said softly. "I'm sorry I hurt you in the process."

He was silent for the longest time. Unmoving until he pulled out the chair beside her and sat down. "Why did you turn... Is that the right term? Turned?"

She shrugged. "Turned. Sired. Whichever it is, I made Ryder a vampire."

"Because..." he said and motioned with his one hand for her to continue.

"He was kind to me. And to my daughter. I named her Artemis." Tears came to her eyes as she remembered the day they'd buried the daughter who'd died before she'd had a chance to live. "I dressed her in the clothes I'd made for her baptism. Ryder had one of his hands build a beautiful little casket lined with pink satin. It was so soft as I laid Artemis in it. A comfortable place for her to rest."

Swiping at the tears trailing down her face, she continued. "There was this rise overlooking the river by Ryder's plantation. An idyllic spot right next to a cherry tree. We buried her there."

Peter held back his questions, but did nothing else to comfort her. What she deserved, she supposed, given the way she'd treated him. She couldn't expect his kindness any longer. Determined that he know everything, she finished her story.

"After, I went home. Elias didn't come around for days. When he did, he was in a mood I'd never seen before. He didn't want me again after the baby, not like a husband wants a wife. The things he made me do... It wasn't enough to make me feel like a whore I guess, 'cause he took to whipping me with a switch."

That would explain so many things, including the marks on her back, Peter thought. "You told me before that you didn't kill him. Was that a lie as well?"

Her head shot up. "No, it wasn't. He was killed in a card game. But I didn't shed a tear at his passing."

He nodded, but knew her story was far from complete. "Who sired you?"

"A stranger who attacked me one night while I was running an errand for the Danvers family."

"Melissa Danvers? Ryder's…keeper, I suppose." It was hard for him to imagine the young doctor as Ryder's protector.

Samantha shrugged, nervously clasping and unclasping her hands. "I don't know a Melissa, but she could be a descendant of Ryder's friend. He was a decent man and kind to me. I was getting some medicine for his sick baby when I was grabbed."

"That's when this vampire…turned you?" Peter asked.

"No. First he raped me. I could have survived that. In retrospect, Elias had been raping me for a long time. My attacker decided he liked my spirit and wanted to keep me around for his enjoyment."

This time, Peter couldn't refrain from placing his hand over hers in a comforting gesture. "I'm sorry."

She pulled her hands away and slipped them beneath the table. "I'd rather your hate than your pity, Peter."

He examined her at length and found that some of the spirit he'd first seen in her had returned. Telling her story had helped somehow. "Hate like Ryder holds against you for killing him?"

What little color she had in her face fled. "I didn't kill him. Ryder was already almost dead. The only way I could save him was to make him like me."

"Without his consent?"

She hesitated and then turned away. Staring at a far wall, it was almost as if she was seeing that night once again. Or at least it seemed that way to him, for her voice had a faraway sound when she told him what happened.

"I thought I could help him." There was true anguish on her face. Tears filled her eyes and she bit her lower lip, worrying the scar there in a gesture that had become too familiar to him.

"Why?"

"He told me he didn't want to die. I believed him and—"

"Made him like you," Peter finished for her. "Have you sired others?"

She shook her head. "No."

"But you feed on humans? That's what you and your friends do down at The Blood Bank?"

"I feed on blood bags and cow's blood from a local butcher normally." She looked down at the surface of the table, avoiding his gaze.

Her answer wasn't enough. "And not normally? What do you do then?"

She remained silent until he moved closer, silently urging her to answer.

"I've fed on Diego. After the shooting when I was hurt, I needed to regain my strength. And sometimes, but rarely, if there's a willing human…"

What was he still doing here, talking to a blood-sucking vampire? Why had he asked Diana to wait for him, as if he could really help Samantha and her undead friends? Only it wasn't just Samantha and her vampires. It was also the women and children in the shelter, who'd be in trouble with Samantha gone. And the others in the neighborhood, who had benefited from Samantha's presence. And his friend Diana, who for some reason he couldn't fathom, was in love with a vampire. One who might be next on the kidnapper's list.

But after he finished listing all the reasons he was still here, he realized there was one reason he didn't want to consider—

he still had some feelings for Samantha even after tonight's discovery. Not that he wanted to. Not that it made sense. It didn't. She was a vampire who existed in a world unlike any he could imagine. A demon whose very nature was one of violence, no matter how many good deeds Samantha did to balance the scales. Which meant that once he was done helping the others, he would have no choice but to leave her. He had too much violence in his life as it was.

"To be honest, although that is something you know so little about," he began, forcing anger into his voice to hide his conflicting emotions, "I don't care what happens to you or your toothy friends, Ryder included. But I do care about the women and kids here and about my friend, Diana."

"Which means what, Peter?" She inclined her head in a regal gesture meant to let him know his words hadn't harmed her.

"That I'll help Diana figure out what's happening."

"And after? Once we know?"

He told himself not to listen to the hopeful tone in her voice. It only created more conflict within him.

"After? I'm outta here," he replied in as cold a tone as he could muster. A tone he hoped would not only convince her of his intentions, but convince him as well.

He saw the life go out of her eyes as they turned a dull dead gray. She bit her lower lip and nodded. "Understood. So where do we begin?"

Chapter 18

Investigating three missing vampires wasn't much different from any other kind of missing persons investigation. Except for the who-sired-who part, which was as complicated as a daytime soap opera.

Peter tried to distance himself from that aspect as well as the whole we're-trying-to-find-a-bunch-of-missing-vampires thing. It was easier if he thought of them as people. Regular everyday humans.

Diana sat beside him in his sedan, on their way to The Blood Bank. Was distance how *she* handled it? "Ryder and you," he began, gripping the wheel tightly as uneasiness ripped through him.

"Are involved. I know that's hard for you to grasp."

"You're wearing a cross." He nodded his head at the gleaming golden crucifix around her neck.

Diana held it in her hand. "It doesn't affect him. Maybe because I don't believe the way I should."

"Sometimes in our line of work, it's hard to believe there's a God. I mean, why let innocents suffer while the evil ones go free?" he said with a careless shrug.

"Or why punish someone like Samantha? Seems to me the men who did this to her never received the punishment they deserved."

Silence was his only answer. This wasn't the first time he'd questioned why Samantha's husband hadn't paid for his crimes. And had the vampire who raped and sired her paid for those evil acts?

So maybe Samantha deserved to be punished for what she had done to Ryder. The fact that Ryder wasn't here, helping them, was proof that he hadn't forgiven her.

Could Peter forgive her? First she had deceived him about her role in the shooting, and after, about what she was. Worse yet, he had broken his own rules about women and placed his trust in her. Even sought out a relationship. Just like before, that relationship—as brief as it had been—had left him hurt and disillusioned.

He wasn't sure he could forgive her that. And he wondered how long it would take to forget her.

As he turned off the FDR and drove through the smaller and less orderly streets of downtown Manhattan, he told himself that once this investigation was over, time away from her would help him forget. Although he wasn't sure he could ever walk in the night again without thinking that a vampire might be lurking nearby.

After a few more twists and turns, Peter pulled the car onto one of the older cobblestone streets. The tires made a *thu-thump* noise against the uneven pavement.

"Just a little bit farther. Right into that alley," Diana said, glancing down at a small slip of paper.

"Directions?"

"Ryder gave them to me."

When he approached the small alleyway and turned, he realized they wouldn't need the directions anymore. Halfway down the narrow passage, Ryder leaned against the wall of one building. Beside him, a short line of people were waiting by a door guarded by a rather large and heavily muscled man.

The alley was too tight for him to park the car, so he backed it out the few feet and stationed it on the main road.

"I didn't think you were helping us," Diana said to her lover as they approached. Her breath marked the chill night air.

Ryder shot an unfriendly glance at Peter. "They won't let just anyone into the club. Especially him," he said and inclined his head in Peter's direction.

Diana shot Ryder a puzzled look.

"Darlin', you've been marked by my bite, but him…" Ryder leaned over and sniffed Peter. "He smells of goodness and light and everything nice," he said derisively.

"Down boy," Diana warned. "I'm sorry, Peter."

"The only thing I'm sorry about is being dragged into Samantha's problems once more." Ryder held his hand toward the door.

The bouncer hesitated, until Ryder began to change, his eyes glowing brightly. In response, the bouncer showed a hint of his true face and pulled aside the velvet rope to let them pass.

Inside it was crowded. Goths of assorted shapes and sizes, looking decidedly similar with their artificially white faces and overdone black clothing. Other, rougher-looking individuals, some who snarled as they walked by, displaying pointy incisors. Last but not least, the more normal-looking characters. Peter suspected they were the ones you had to worry about the most. Their lack of affectation probably spoke to the fact that they were the real thing.

Ryder, Diana and he were all dressed like the real thing. Jeans and dark-colored shirts. Black leather to round out their ensembles, although with his fair hair and tan, he stuck out like a sore thumb next to Diana and Ryder with their dark good looks.

As they walked through the crowd, Peter kept a lookout for the missing vamps. Diana had obtained a picture of Meghan from her high school yearbook and a missing persons report her parents had filed nearly a year earlier. A pretty girl in that All-American cheerleader kind of way. It made him wonder why she'd ever visited this club.

The photo of the other female vampire, Esperanza, had come from her lover, Diego, who was safely tucked away in his lair, protected by his keeper.

The last vampire might be harder to locate. No one had any pictures of Blake, although both Diego and Samantha had offered the same description—look for a Billy Idol clone who was a natural towhead.

So far, Peter had seen no one even remotely matching the descriptions of the three missing vampires.

Past the crowd congregating on the dance floor, there were tables and booths. Even midweek most of them were occupied, but eventually they located a small booth in the back of the club, and Ryder waved to a waitress.

"The freshest for me," Ryder said.

The waitress shook her head and put down her pad. "You must be new here, otherwise you'd know we don't just serve anyone—"

Ryder transformed, showing her a bit of fang and skewering her with his almost electric gaze.

The girl allowed herself to morph a bit before quickly noting his request.

"Cuervo shooter," Diana said. Peter copied her order and the waitress left, returning a short time later with the drinks. She placed before them the two shooters and a shot glass with a dark cherry liquid that had to be the blood. Peter wondered where it came from, but that thought was quickly replaced by his need to control the urge to gag as Ryder sipped his drink.

Diana seemed to have no such problem. She picked up the Cuervo and held it up to him, as if in a toast. *"Salud."*

Peter downed the tequila, letting it drive away the imaginary taste of blood that lingered in his mouth. "What do we do now?"

Once again he examined the crowd in the club, but there was no one who matched the descriptions of Esperanza and Blake, and one too many young girls who matched Meghan's type.

"We try to fit in. See who has information," Diana explained.

"They won't talk to a vampire they don't know, much less a human," Samantha said as she appeared in an abrupt blur of motion beside their booth.

Peter popped out of his seat at her unexpected appearance. "How did you get here? But more importantly, *why* are you here?"

"Vamp speed," she answered in response to his first question. She motioned for him to sit back down. "As for the 'Why?', my friends are missing and I want to help."

"You might be in danger here." He shot a look around the club to see if anyone seemed more interested in them now that Samantha had arrived. Everything was as it had been before.

"I thought you didn't care," she said in challenge as she sat beside him.

At her comment, Diana gave a strangled laugh, rose and held her hand out to Ryder. "I think it's time we went for a dance."

"Darlin', you know what that does to me." His voice had a low edge of darkness in it as he laid a hand at her waist and bent to nuzzle her neck.

"Easy, Ryder. At least for now." She gave the vampire a playful shrug.

Placing her hands on the edge of the table, she leaned forward and in a voice soft enough so only the occupants of their booth could hear said, "I expect now that Samantha's arrived, we'll have a visit. But don't do anything until we return."

With that, she grabbed Ryder's hand and dragged him to the dance floor. Once again Ryder staked his claim on her, wrapping an arm around her waist and bending his head to be almost one with her. The dark strands of his hair merged with Diana's, their faces pressed together.

"Diana and Ryder are very…interesting," Samantha said as she watched them. The affection between the two was obvious and disconcerting. It reminded her all too painfully of what she would never experience with the man sitting beside her.

"I guess you can say that." His tone was uneasy.

Samantha examined him carefully in the dim light. Despite the darkness, the kiss of the sun in his hair and on his skin was visibly alive. Vibrant. The heat of him called to her as she remembered what it was like to be held against that warmth. She laid her hand over his and when he didn't pull away, said, "I don't know how to thank you."

Peter forced himself to meet her gaze. Her all-too-human gaze, which remained capable of starting a weird feeling in the area of his heart. It gave him pause until the chill of her skin reminded him that any emotion for her was a mistake.

"Like I said before, it's not you and your friends I'm trying to protect."

Her skin paled and her eyes grew a turbulent gray before she looked back to the dance floor where Ryder and Diana were kissing intimately as they danced. If you could call that dancing, she thought. Their excitement carried all the way to the booth.

"Are those your friends?" someone asked and Peter whipped his head up, having been so engrossed in watching Diana and Ryder that he'd failed to notice the appearance of the tall man standing before him. Vamp speed again.

The vamp was dressed in what was clearly a very expensive suit. A dark charcoal-gray, like his shirt. It only served to make the paleness of his skin and his nearly white hair seem even more striking. And there was something about him, some thrum of energy coming off his body that confirmed he wasn't human.

"Blake?" Peter asked, although this man's dress was richly elegant and not remotely punk.

Before Peter could react, his throat was in a viselike grip and he was roughly yanked from his seat. Grabbing at the man's hand, he struggled for air.

The vampire brought his face directly into Peter's line of sight. Clear gray eyes burned with an icy fire. When he spoke, there was a rumble in his voice, like the sound of an approaching summer storm. "You insult me with that question."

Samantha shot out of her seat, grabbed hold of the vampire's wrist and immediately transformed into a demon. Her voice had a low ominous reverberation as she commanded, "Let him go, Foley."

The vampire relaxed his grip slightly. Peter was thankful for even that small respite from the punishing hold.

"So Little Miss Goody Two-shoes has some bite after all."

Like someone might toss a rag doll, the vampire threw him

back onto the booth. Peter rubbed his abused throat as Samantha sat beside him. "Are you okay?" she asked.

She was still in vamp mode. Peter found himself both fascinated and repelled by her appearance. She must have sensed the latter, for she immediately reverted to her human state.

A second later, Diana and Ryder returned and the vampire turned his attention to them. "Is this sorry human your keeper?" After a quizzical look he positioned a hand above Diana's center and said, "You're not one of us."

Without missing a beat, he turned to Ryder. "You violate our rules by being with her."

Rules? There were frickin' rules to being a vampire? Peter anxiously awaited Ryder's response, fearing things might get out of control.

With considerable restraint, Ryder bowed his head and kept it bowed. "I'm new to this. I didn't know there were rules."

The other vampire placed his hand above Ryder's heart, much as he had done with Diana. After a moment, he said, "Your energy is too strong for you to be newly turned."

"He's new to acknowledging what he is," Samantha said.

The vampire laughed harshly. "Another of the human wannabes. Do you belong to Diego's band?"

"I belong to only one person," Ryder responded. To stress that point, he slipped his hand into Diana's and she in turn, leaned into his side.

Shock crossed the vampire's face, followed by amusement. He examined Diana carefully, eyeing her from head to toe before nodding. "I can understand your fascination, my friend. For a human, the darkness is strong within her."

"If you're done with your little inspection, we're here because we may need your help." Diana motioned for the vampire to take a seat at the booth.

Chapter 19

He seated himself between the two women, forcing Peter and Ryder to sit beside each other. Then he introduced himself. "They call me Foley. I own this bar and most of the vampires within it follow me."

"Foley? First name or last?" Peter questioned.

"Just Foley."

Peter was growing a little tired of the arrogance of these creatures. "Just Foley. Kind of like Cher or Madonna. Very eighties of you."

Foley laughed, surprising them all. "Yes, it is very eighties of me. 1780s to be more precise."

"Your age being what makes you the leader of the vampires here?" Ryder asked and once again the other vampire cackled with amusement.

"You *are* rather new to this, aren't you?" Foley raised his hand and signaled for the waitress, who immediately hurried over. "Another round here. On the house."

She scurried away at the negligent wave of his hand. If not for the slightly longer nails, which made him seem somewhat effeminate, it was a pale but perfectly normal-looking hand. But Peter knew the strength those longish fingers were capable of. He rubbed his sore throat and suspected he bore marks from the vampire's grip.

After the vampire waitress had brought fresh shots of blood and tequila, Foley continued. "I hear you're looking for Diego's missing friends. What can I do to help?"

Peter rocked backward at the statement. Surprise was stamped on the faces of Diana, Ryder and even Samantha. "It can't possibly be that easy," he said.

"Oh, but it is. Rumor has it someone's vampire hunting and some of my clientele is taking that threat very seriously. Vamp business is off and when that happens, the rest of the business suffers as well."

Ryder observed the crowd, which was still fairly large. "Because your human clientele—"

"Wants to imagine that they're surrounded by the real thing. If they didn't, they'd go somewhere like The Lair. That's your place, isn't it?" A slight sneer came to Foley's lips, but it didn't get a rise from Ryder.

He gave a careless shrug, followed by, "Because being around our kind—"

"Is a rush. These humans sense our power and imagine that we will be foolish enough to share it with them." Foley took a sip from his shot glass of blood, which once again forced Peter to toss down his tequila to avoid gagging.

Diana jumped into the discussion. "You don't allow that here?"

"Not normally. It raises too many questions and that risks our existence. The freedom we have here."

"But Blake sired Meghan?" Ryder asked, prompting a harsh laugh from Foley and a quick interjection from Samantha.

"Sometimes it happens. Blake was always—"

"A sorry bloke. We warned him that if he did it again, we'd finish him ourselves and he listened. But Meghan became a problem." Foley finished his drink and smacked his lips with pleasure. A slight bit of fang was visible as he did so, but he quickly retracted them to appear fully human once more.

"Is it possible one of the other vampires decided to deal with the Blake-Meghan problem?" Peter asked, thinking that in the human world, that was the most plausible of explanations.

Foley shrugged and the jacket of his suit stretched across wide, but thin shoulders. "Easy enough to do. A quick twist of the neck. Rip the throat out for a bit more fun." He mimicked both actions with his hands.

Diana was seemingly unperturbed by Foley's bloodthirsty response. "But the bodies—"

"Would just shrivel up and blow away. Once seriously injured or dead, vampire bodies are quite fragile things," Samantha said and then launched into a more detailed explanation. "First the sweats drain the body of its life fluids until what remains is bone, muscle and sinew."

At that, Diana looked over at Ryder. Peter surmised that Ryder must have been in such a state at one time. He didn't want to think about what Diana had done to help him recover.

Samantha shot an uncomfortable glance at Ryder and Diana, then at Peter. "A vampire in that final state is often like a mummy. After, what remains of the body slowly loses the last of its moisture and becomes nothing more than ash."

"Ashes to ashes. Dust to dust," Foley replied cynically.

Peter's mind was racing as he tried to take it all in. "From start to finish this would take?"

Samantha paused for a moment, considering. "Less than a day. Especially if the body was left out in the sun."

"So it's possible Blake and Meghan are now—"

"Dust in the wind," Diana finished for him. "Why do you think it wasn't someone here?"

"They might think of ridding the group of the two problem vampires, but not Esperanza. There are few who would risk Diego's wrath," Foley answered without hesitation and signaled the waitress again for another round.

Peter had yet to meet Diego, but found himself suddenly more anxious to do so. The elusive vampire was the one who'd been calling Samantha and with whom she clearly had some kind of relationship. He told himself it wasn't jealousy driving him, but curiosity about someone the others feared. "So if only a few would dare—"

"Only a few, but who knows what one might dare for the right temptation," Foley said and stared at Diana.

Unfortunately, Peter understood only too well about temptation and found himself looking at Samantha. Trying to get the conversation back on the right track, he asked, "What else can you tell us?"

"Has anyone new been around?" Diana added.

"An older gentleman. A professorial type."

"How old? Sixties? Seventies?" Peter asked.

"Younger, I believe. I haven't seen him myself. Some of the others have and I'm told he shared a room with Meghan." Foley inclined his head toward the back of the club, where a curtain and bouncer marked off an area with private rooms.

"Why would she go with him?" Samantha asked.

Foley shrugged and rose abruptly, as if he'd had enough of

their company. "Ask your questions and then leave. And if at all possible, don't come back." The last statement was clearly directed at Ryder. Did Foley see Ryder as a threat to his authority or was it about something else—like maybe Diana?

"We'll be back until we've got the answers we need, Foley. If you want this little piece of Hell to stay in business, you won't stop us," Ryder stood almost nose to nose with Foley.

They were of a like height, but Ryder was more heavily muscled and fit. Foley seemed insubstantial next to him and he must have realized it, for he backed away, Ryder's show of power having accomplished just what he wanted. "Do what you must and then stay away."

With a gracious nod, Ryder said, "Thank you for your hospitality."

Diana slipped between the two vampires and with a subtle push, moved Ryder back just a bit. "Thank you, Foley. If you don't mind, we're going to ask around."

Peter admired her chutzpah while at the same time worrying about what his friend had involved herself in. For that matter, he thought about what *he* had signed up for. Whatever was going on, it was clearly for keeps. He suspected that the three missing vamps were probably big piles of dust by now. But if they weren't...

He rose and motioned to the private rooms. "Mind if I check them out?" He took a step toward them, but Foley placed a hand in the middle of his chest to hold him back.

"Couples only," Foley said. Samantha uneasily averted her gaze, leaving only one possibility.

Diana glanced at Ryder. "*Amor,* do you mind?"

Amusement flared in his eyes as he said, "It's a tough job, but someone's got to do it."

A schoolgirl flush passed over Diana's cheeks. It surprised

Peter, so much so that he forgot to ask what they wanted him to do while they were in the back. But Diana paused at his side and said, "Maybe Foley or Samantha can introduce you to the others."

"Right," he agreed. Interview the little bloodsuckers and hope they don't take a liking to my neck.

"Don't worry. They won't bite," Foley said, as Peter and Samantha headed into the crowd.

Peter had thought himself a good judge of people and surprisingly, that trait was applicable to the undead. He almost didn't need Foley and Samantha to point out the vamps. Whether it was the power and darkness Foley had claimed to feel in Diana, or whether it was a good ol' fashioned read of body language and attitude, Peter could pick them out.

By the time he and Samantha had spoken to the sixth vamp that night, he wondered why he wasn't picking up similar vibes from either Samantha or Ryder. Even after they'd finished their interviews and were once again sitting at the booth, she seemed more human than her undead counterparts. Maybe because, unlike those other vamps, who relished what immortal life provided them, Samantha and Ryder preferred a more human existence—wannabes. At least that's the way the other vamps thought of them.

The interviews confirmed what Foley had told them. Meghan had been spotted with a man in his mid-fifties. Tweedy-type with gray hair. The description reminded Peter of Edward Sloan the villain involved in the Danvers' case last year. The man, another professor-type with an unhealthy interest in vampires had died in a warehouse fire. The similarities between Sloan and this fifty-something could only be coincidence.

As for why Meghan would go into the private rooms with

a man old enough to be her father, the vampires couldn't begin to speculate, other than to say that Meghan hadn't really been of sound mind after being sired. Some even said that if Peter was searching for someone, it should be for the human. When on a binge, Meghan was likely to drain her victims dry.

With Samantha sitting beside him, awkward and silent, Peter flipped through his notes while they waited for Diana and Ryder to return. It had been close to an hour since the two had disappeared into the private rooms. Peter could only guess at what they were up to in addition to investigating. Samantha, too, seemed to have the same idea about what was keeping his friends.

Their guess was confirmed a few minutes later when Ryder and Diana swept from behind the curtain, arm in arm with broad smiles. Diana even giggled as Ryder whispered something into her ear.

When the two arrived at the table, the purpling mark—a human love bite—on Diana's neck was obvious thanks to her halter blouse. He shot a quick glance at Ryder. There was nothing vamp about him. "Did you have a…productive time back there?"

That telltale flush erupted on Diana's face again and, surprisingly, on Ryder's as well. *Undead immortals could blush.* What would it take to make Samantha blush?

He wouldn't take that thought any further. There was *not* going to be anything between himself and Samantha. Not ever again. Unfortunately the vehemence of that thought brought the truth to mind: *Methinks you doth protest too much.*

Diana was the first to answer his query. "There're several vamps who take turns watching the back rooms. The guard on duty tonight was there when Blake turned Meghan."

"And he was also there when Meghan left with the professor," Ryder added.

"Why would Meghan go with a stranger?" Peter asked.

Samantha shrugged. "After one of her 'living in the light' phases, she'd be out of control with the need to feed."

"Meaning?" Peter asked calmly.

"To keep control, you need to keep regular—"

"Blood being Metamucil for the undead?" he retorted, clearly unnerved by the whole concept.

"Blood being about life," Ryder clarified from across the length of the table. "Like you, we need it to keep going. To make us warm. To drive the undeadness from us."

Samantha continued with her explanation. "If we go too long without it, the need becomes unbearable. We were always able to restore Meghan by letting her feed on either Diego or Esperanza, but maybe—"

"She decided an old man wouldn't put up much of a fight," Peter finished for her.

"So where's the body? Unlike vamp bodies, human ones linger," Diana interjected. "Plus, as far as we know, when she left the building the old man was alive."

"And someone thinks they saw the old man on the night Blake disappeared," Ryder added.

Samantha considered all they had said, but it wasn't helping at all. "The two men who grabbed me were younger."

"Any luck with that, Peter?" Diana asked.

Peter nodded. "From the plate number the women at the shelter provided, I was able to track down the van this morning. It was towed to an impound lot after being abandoned. The owners in Westchester had reported the van stolen a few nights before. I found a few sets of prints on the van and a friend is running them right now."

After Peter's report it seemed to Samantha that there was no more information to get that night. "I need to get back to the shelter. Maybe we'll have more information from the prints tomorrow."

Ryder laughed harshly. She saw now that the vampire's mood had turned ugly. "What makes you think I'll help you anymore?"

She and Peter shared a quick glance before Diana placed her hand over Ryder's chest. "You promised."

Ryder twined his fingers with hers. "Darlin', I will be on my best behavior. But don't think that I'd regret it if Ms. Turner here got a little payback for what she did to me."

"Don't you think Samantha's suffered enough in her life?" Peter grabbed Samantha's hand and led her toward the exit. As she walked away, Ryder's gaze bored holes in the middle of her back, but she ignored it. Instead she concentrated on the feel of Peter's hand in hers, took hope in the fact that he had come to her defense.

In the alley outside the club, they walked side by side in silence, and they still didn't say anything as Peter drove her back to the shelter. Once he'd parked, he shut off the engine and they sat there quietly, as if taking in all that had happened tonight and all that hadn't.

He wasn't looking her way. He was staring straight ahead, his hands wrapped tightly around the steering wheel. His body stiff and unyielding. Around his throat, bruises were blossoming from Foley's attack.

"I'm sorry you were hurt," she whispered, hoping to somehow reach him.

He chuckled, but it was a harsh sound. "Considering that in the past few days I've been hit by a Taser, nearly strangled, and have had my heart broken, 'sorry' doesn't quite seem to cut it."

She wanted to say more, but he didn't give her a chance. With a sharp slash of his hand, he motioned for her to go.

Samantha stepped out of the car and shut the door. The wheels squealed as he peeled away.

Samantha took a weary step toward the shelter, but knew it would give her no comfort. Whirling, she raced into the night, trying to distance herself from the maelstrom of feelings roiling within her heart.

Chapter 20

It was hard to get to sleep. First, there was his sore throat, which reminded him of vampires every time he swallowed. Second, the concern that such soreness was minor compared to what Foley or the others he'd met that night could do. Third, and finally, annoyingly, Samantha.

He had every right to be angry. First the Taser. Second his throat. Third, and most importantly, her lying to him about something so important. On the rank of things that one prospective lover told another—like being married, safe or on the kinky side—"Hi, I'm a vampire" might actually be *numero uno*.

As he lay staring up at the ceiling, his hands pillowed behind his head, he wondered how he might have reacted if Samantha had told him.

He likely would not have believed her. He might even have thought her totally crazy.

The insane thing was, he probably would have ignored

that craziness because…Samantha intrigued him. She presented such a competent and able facade, but within, she was still badly wounded. It was those wounds that had propelled her into a life of helping others. From what he could see of the women and children in the shelter, and of the blocks surrounding the shelter, Samantha had accomplished a lot of good in her life.

Her undead life.

Which prompted him to sneak a look at the shadows in his bedroom. The same old darkness, except for the slight breeze shifting the pale pink chiffon curtains his wife had hung. *An open window.*

His neck and throat complained again—loudly—as he went to the window to close it. Something shifted on the fire escape, prompting him to pull aside the curtain and peer into the night.

Nothing.

It had probably been his overworked imagination. Closing the window and locking it for good measure, he padded back to bed, shivering. The spring breeze still had the bite of winter in it.

Or at least that's what he told himself. He was a grown man after all and shouldn't be afraid of things that go bump in the night.

Especially when those things appeared as attractive as Samantha. Tasted as good. Felt as wonderful pressed against him.

The shiver of cold and fear was replaced with one of desire as he slipped beneath the sheets. Not good. It was foolish to still be thinking about her that way.

Having sworn off serious relationships thanks to his wife, it had been a long time since he'd listed the pros and cons of a prospective date. In his past few dalliances, the only pros he'd considered were that the woman was willing and uninterested in any kind of lasting involvement.

That had worked to satisfy the urge for sex when it came.

Somehow, whatever had been going on with Samantha was about more than the sex, violating his Golden Rule about getting involved. But since he'd already broken that rule…

Pro number one: Her smile did something to him that made his stomach do little flip-flops and, right now, brought a twitch of life to places he didn't need coming alive tonight.

Pro number two: She was mentally strong. Seemingly capable of handling anything.

The sad upshot of that pro was that her strength came from the harsh trials she'd been forced to face. Although he suspected her courage had always been there, ready to be used.

Pro number three: She was beautiful, oh-so-amazingly gorgeous. He loved the way the mass of her dark hair framed her face. Her skin the color of fresh cream touched by coffee. Or chocolate.

Yes, white chocolate, considering how her lips and breasts had tasted.

He groaned as his nether regions came fully to life. He reached beneath the sheets and grabbed himself. Stroked slowly, ignoring the discomfort in his throat and neck, which should have reminded him that his desire for her could bring him nothing but pain.

But it was hard to forget her as he remembered the fullness of her breasts and how they'd fit perfectly in his hand. How he had licked and sucked at the tips during their one and only encounter.

Pro number four: her passion. He'd roused but the beginning of it that night and it had still been more than he'd ever experienced with any other woman.

Passion like nothing else. Passion with the power to make him forget about everything except...

Con number one, which quashed the desire snaking through him more effectively than an ice-cold shower. He lay there, breathing heavily. His body damp and his needs unfulfilled thanks to the biggest and most overwhelming of cons.

Con number one: Vampire. Blood-sucking, throat-ripping, life-ending vampire.

He much preferred thinking of all the pros. He'd go back to the top of the list and take it a little more slowly this time.

The night air was chill and filled with damp from a spring rain. It was the kind of weather that seeped into your bones. If you were human, of course.

To vampires things like hot and cold had totally different meanings. Although maybe they weren't that different, Samantha thought now. Much as humans craved warmth, vampires thrived on the heat within them, searing them from inside through their transformation. Bringing with it super-human powers, lusts and cravings.

Unlike the cold that cloaked them during the day and when their human forms took control.

Samantha much preferred the cold.

It was why she was impervious to the night's chill as she crouched behind the ledge of the building across from Peter's, watching. Struggling to catch sight of him. It had been easier when she'd been on the fire escape.

He must have caught a glimpse of her spying on him, for he'd come to the window. She'd had to beat a hasty retreat to the building across the way.

It had been a while, however, since his earlier appearance at the window. Maybe long enough for her to return to her perch and…

Why was she here? Why had she come to see him? He'd made it quite clear how he felt. How he held her responsible for so many of his hurts.

Maybe that was why she sat on the ledge, watching his building. Seeing no activity from his apartment, she decided to return to the fire escape. To watch him and make sure he was safe.

She walked a few yards away from the ledge of the building. As much as she liked the cold of her human body and what it signified, she knew she needed more strength to make the jump. Arms outspread, her head turned up to the skies, she fixed her gaze on the murky moon, partially obscured by rain clouds. Reaching deep within her, she sought out the demon, sensed it wake, warm and willing to be free.

The heat grew and power singed her nerve endings, wakening every sense. The light of the moon became brighter as vampire sight took over. With a deep breath, she sucked in the smells of the city at night, the freshness of things washed clean by the rain.

Lowering her gaze, she focused on the opposite ledge and rushed toward it, leaping. She landed on two feet, agile as a cat. Carefully she slipped over the ledge and controlled her fall. When she landed on the fire escape, it was noiseless.

Although his window was closed, he'd been careless when shutting it. A piece of curtain was trapped at the bottom, creating a small opening through which she could see him.

He was lying partially beneath the sheets, most of his body exposed. He was naked. With her heightened vision, she could see every wonderful inch despite the darkness of the night. The strong muscles of his arms. The firm planes of his chest.

The heat within her increased, both human and vampire responding to her desire for the man beyond the glass.

She had chastised herself often during the last few days. She should forget her feelings for him. Forget the delicious way he made her want to be alive again, like a real woman once more.

Forgetting had seemed nearly impossible until his reminder that the only thing she'd brought into his life had been pain.

In her mind's eye, she recollected the marks left on him by the Taser. As she observed him now, the painful red imprint of Foley's hand was vivid against his throat. His throat, where his pulse beat, growing more rapid as she watched.

Her heart raced along with his. Too fast. Too erratic it occurred to her. She searched out the reason and seeing why, she groaned and fell back against the edge of the fire escape.

She should leave. Yet she couldn't drag herself away from the sight of him. From surreptitiously feeding on his rising passion.

As she crouched there, ensnared by what he was doing, she remembered how it had been with them. How the muscles of his chest had been hard when pressed against hers, while his skin had been oh-so-soft and warm. How he had licked and sucked…

She moaned as her body sprang to life, joining him on his journey. It was all she could do to stop herself from breaking through that window and slipping into bed beside him to savor the warmth of his body as passion grew, smell the damp of their arousal, strong as her body responded and demanded she find completion.

Sexual completion. She ran one hand over her hard nipples. She imagined his mouth on them, pleasuring her.

Vampire completion. She passed her other hand over the fangs that had erupted along with her human passion. Just as they almost had the other night. There was but one way to satisfy this urge, only she couldn't—wouldn't—do that to Peter.

With a strangled groan, she gave him one last look, and then threw herself over the edge of the fire escape.

She hit the ground running and didn't stop, knowing she had to tire out the vampire within if she had any hope of being normal by the time morning came and, with it, all her human responsibilities.

I'm sorry, Peter.

She ran as if chased by the hounds of hell. Only there was no respite from their pursuit. No safe place where she could avoid the message they sent to her all night long—*Sorry doesn't quite cut it.*

Chapter 21

Days passed without him seeing her. Without any kind of break in the case. The prints had been a dead end. Although two of the sets were in the system, the files were classified and Peter lacked the necessary security clearance.

Of course, when they'd worked on the Sloan case parts of his file had been classified as well, but that hadn't stopped Diana from obtaining the information. He was about to pick up the phone to call her, when one of his buddies yelled, "Hey, Daly. Call for you on line five."

"Daly," he said as he answered the phone.

"Peter, it's Samantha." As if he wouldn't have recognized her voice.

He tried to keep his tone neutral. Without anger. Without excitement. "What's up?"

"Diego's missing."

"And how do you know that?"

There was a moment's hesitation on the line and Peter suspected he wouldn't like the answer to her question. "I've been trying to reach him all day—"

"Because you all like to rise and shine with the sun," he said caustically. "So when he didn't answer—"

"Diego's keeper, Simon, didn't answer. Diego lives on a vampire schedule," she explained, a tinge of annoyance in her voice that he kind of liked. It said she wasn't afraid to stand up to him.

"So you—"

"Went over this afternoon once the sun was weaker. Neither Simon or Diego are there. At least, not that I can tell without going through the apartment."

He imagined her traipsing through the area, possibly destroying evidence in her haste to find her friend or his keeper. "Are you in the apartment?"

"No. I'm in a nearby coffeehouse with plenty of people nearby."

Smart girl. "Stay put. My shift is almost over. While I can't call in CSU, maybe Diana and I can collect evidence on our own." He tucked the phone between his shoulder and ear, and pulled out his notepad. "What's the address of the coffeehouse?"

He wrote it down, then said, "Don't move until we get there."

Samantha slipped the key into the dead bolt and unlocked the door to Diego's apartment. She entered, followed by Peter, Diana and Ryder. She hadn't expected Ryder to help out. She suspected he was doing it solely because of Diana, but didn't really care, if it would assist in finding her missing friends.

She waited by the door, Ryder an unlikely companion beside her, as Diana and Peter swept through Diego's home, scoping out the slightly askew coffee table and upended chair. Moving to the overturned lamp on a sofa side table. Beside the chair and lamp were Simon's walking sticks and a novel.

Peter removed some kind of kit from his jacket and dusted down the lamp.

"There." Diana motioned to something on the base of the lamp. Peter removed a small card, peeled off the backing and took a sample off the lamp.

Those few out of sync things were the only signs of a struggle. Maybe she'd made a mistake in thinking Diego had been taken. Maybe he'd just decided to leave town until things were safer.

Only she couldn't imagine Diego running with Esperanza still missing. Nor would his keeper, Simon, go anywhere without his walking sticks. Simon's legs and hips had been crushed during the 1906 San Francisco earthquake. Diego found Simon in the wreckage, but hadn't been able to completely heal him after saving his life.

Diana and Peter continued searching the apartment until they'd reached the door to the farthest room. "Is this where Diego…sleeps?" Peter asked.

She nodded.

"Where is Diego's keeper normally?" Diana asked. "In his own room? In the kitchen?"

"In that easy chair," Samantha answered and pointed to the upended chair in the other room. "Simon doesn't get around too well, so once he's up and about, he generally settles there to either read or watch television."

Once they were all standing in the bedroom, Peter asked, "Anything out of place?"

"I've never been in here before."

A pleased smile crossed Peter's face before he could con-

trol it, but that pleasure was short-lived as a barely discerna-
ble thump caught the attention of all of them.

Ryder was the first to act. He strode quickly to a nearby
closet and after laying his head against one of the sliding
doors, opened it.

On the floor, trussed up and gagged was Simon. The
thumping had been him desperately banging his head against
the wall to get their attention.

At the sight of Ryder, Simon grew more agitated. His eyes
were wild-looking and he pressed his heels into the floor, trying to push himself farther against the wall.

Samantha cursed beneath her breath. She urged Ryder
away from the nearly frantic Simon. While lowering the gag
and untying his hands, she said in soft tones, "It's okay,
Simon. These are friends."

Simon shook his head, his gaze fixed straight ahead to the
other side of the wide closet. "Esperanza," he whispered and
again pushed with his heels against the floor, as if trying to
escape.

Samantha peered into the closet. The sight within made her
lurch back. She lost her balance and landed on her butt.
Reaching into the closet, she dragged Simon out and closed
the door.

Peter was at her side in a heartbeat. "What's wrong? What
did you see?"

She met his worried gaze. "It's Esperanza. On the other
side of the closet. Or what's left of her."

At her words, Ryder slowly slid the other door open to reveal the nearly desiccated corpse of the female vampire.

His and Peter's reactions were as immediate as hers. Both
of them reeled back, gaping at the shriveled remains.
Esperanza was just a pile of skin and bone. If not for the dis-

tinctive long auburn hair that clung to what remained of her head, it would have been hard to identify her mummylike features.

Beside her, Simon's keening became a loud wail and she tried to comfort him. "It's okay, Simon. We'll take care of everything."

"They took Diego. They'll kill him, too!"

Diana kneeled beside Samantha and the old man. "We will find him, Simon. But we'll need your help."

Vehemently, Simon shook his head. "They'll kill me, too. Because I'm his keeper."

"No, Simon. They won't. We'll make sure of that," Samantha said, but Simon was too far gone to listen to reason.

Samantha met Diana's gaze. "We need to get him out of here. Calm him down. See if he's hurt."

Diana nodded and glanced over her shoulder at Ryder. "Can you call Melissa? Ask her to come?"

With a curt nod to signal his agreement, he whipped out his cell phone, but walked out of the room for privacy.

Diana returned her attention to Simon. "Can we move him into the other room?"

In human form, she'd barely be able to budge Simon. Before she could vamp out for the extra strength, Peter came to her side. "I can help."

Between the two of them, they carried Simon to the living room, where they settled him on the sofa. As soon as the old man was lying down, he began babbling again.

She placed a blanket over Simon and tried to calm him down. He was clearly in shock and needed to be kept warm. In soft tones, she tried to reassure him. Slowly, the old man's wails and frantic movements subsided. Eventually, he slipped into sleep.

She wrapped her arms around herself tightly. What had

happened? Why had they left Esperanza behind? As a warning or some kind of sick joke?

Peter stood beside her, tension in his body. She could understand why. She'd dragged him into something beyond his wildest imagination. Something she wasn't sure wouldn't get him killed. Or her for that matter.

Esperanza had been taken before Diego. Samantha could only assume Blake and Meghan had already met similar fates. Diego would too unless they could find him in time. And after… It would be her turn.

But regardless of that, she couldn't ask Peter to continue with his investigation and risk his life as well.

She faced him as he stood stiffly beside her. "I'd understand if you left now. You don't need to help anymore."

Chapter 22

Comfort or condemnation. For Peter, the former was a scary proposition. He was fighting a losing battle to avoid his attraction to her. But the latter was just as scary. It grated against his nature to run away from his duty to protect and serve, even if it meant defending a bunch of vampires.

Who was being more inhumane now? he asked himself as he recalled the sight of Esperanza's mummified remains. The vamps or the humans rounding them up?

His answer came almost subconsciously as he laid a hand on Samantha's shoulder. "I'm not running from this until we've stopped whoever is doing it."

Giving him a sidelong glance, she asked, "And after? Will you go after that?"

As he had feared, he couldn't battle the need he saw in her tear-filled eyes or that spark challenging him to what? See her as a woman rather than a vampire?

When he failed to immediately respond, she worried her lower lip in that all too familiar, vulnerable gesture. He cupped her chin and swiped his thumb over her lip.

She turned to face him and he moved his hand to the small of her back. Gently he urged her closer, ignoring everything within him that said run. He wanted to console her, to feel her close to him once again, woman to man.

There was confusion in her gaze and a bit of resistance, but she took a step toward him, laid her head against his chest and wrapped her arms around his waist.

He was about to envelop her in his embrace when a loud grating sound from the intercom intruded. Melissa Danvers had arrived. Not just a doctor but also Ryder's keeper.

Samantha shot him an apologetic look and went to the intercom panel by the front door. She buzzed in Melissa while Peter stood there, awkwardly, knowing the moment they had almost shared was gone.

Diana and Ryder emerged from Diego's bedroom. They shared a compassionate look before Diana said, "We're going to need your help back there to understand what happened."

Samantha nodded. "As soon as Melissa gets here and sees to Simon, I'll join you."

Diana turned her attention to Peter. "Are you ready?"

Peter wanted to ask "Ready for what?" but curbed that impulse. He wasn't sure he was ready for anything. He was confused about his feelings for Samantha. Totally unable to fathom that there really was a world of creatures of the night and he had somehow been sucked into it. And last but not least, he couldn't comprehend that a woman he admired was sleeping with a vampire while the woman he desired *was* a vampire.

"Ready," he said, but with little conviction and a lot of trepidation.

A knock signaled Melissa's arrival.

Samantha opened the door. A petite wisp of a blonde stood beside a handsome young Latino who bore a striking resemblance to Diana. The young man had his arm draped over the beautiful woman's shoulders.

Melissa held out her hand in introduction. "Dr. Melissa Danvers. This is my husband, and Diana's brother, Sebastian Reyes."

A husband? For a keeper? Samantha thought, but refrained from comment. Ryder clearly chose to do things his own way, including allowing his keeper to not only have a spouse, but to maintain her mortality. Vampires usually gifted their keepers with a bit of their strength to prolong their lives without making them vampires. Samantha noticed the lack of transferred vamp power in Melissa's grasp as they shook hands.

Motioning for them to enter, she took them to Simon.

At the sofa, Melissa sat on the coffee table and placed her black doctor's bag next to her. Removing a stethoscope, penlight and blood pressure apparatus, she prepped for examining Diego's keeper. "How old is he?"

Samantha hesitated, not only because she had to recall when Simon had been born, but also because she wasn't sure the young doctor was ready to hear the answer.

Melissa slipped the stethoscope over her neck and leaned toward Simon. She laid a gentle hand on his chest and Simon immediately roused and began his disoriented rambling once more. To Melissa's credit, she quickly calmed the keeper.

Sebastian hovered nearby, within reach of his wife. It was then Samantha noticed his wedding ring with its new and gleaming shine. She noted the same freshly minted glow on

Melissa's wedding band. Guilt flooded her at the thought that she might be bringing the newlyweds into harm's way, especially since Melissa was still mortal.

"Samantha?"

She roused from her musings when Melissa repeated a question she apparently hadn't heard. "I'm sorry. What is it?"

"How old is he?"

There was no avoiding it, especially if Melissa wanted to give Simon any kind of medication. "Simon was born in 1876."

Silence greeted her response until Melissa said, "But he barely looks like he's sixty."

Whether Ryder's omission was intentional or because of his lack of knowledge, Melissa had the right to know. "There are many different kinds of things that vampires can do."

"Meaning?" Sebastian asked. He put a protective hand on Melissa's shoulder.

Samantha tried to explain as best she could. "A vampire can choose to feed or sire someone. Their lick can heal if they want it to."

"And their keepers? What do they do to their keepers?" Melissa asked.

"A different kind of bite, administered as needed." She watched as puzzled looks crossed the faces of both her companions.

"As needed?" Sebastian echoed at the same time that Melissa said, "Could you explain the 'as needed' part?"

With a shrug, she said, "The more frequent the bite, the less the keeper ages."

Once again an awkward silence greeted her words, until Melissa made a little circular motion with one finger and said, "So, a bite a day—"

"Keeps the Reaper away," Sebastian added.

Samantha couldn't contain a chuckle. "I guess that's about as simple an explanation as possible."

Seemingly satisfied, Melissa turned her attention to examining Simon, checking his pulse and blood pressure. Asking him some simple questions to determine if he'd been injured.

Content that Simon was being well-attended, Samantha walked to Diego's bedroom, but paused as she noticed Ryder and Peter carrying something cradled in a sheet. Something that barely made a dent in the center of the fabric.

Away from the closet and in the free floor space before Diego's ornate four-poster bed, Peter and Ryder laid the sheet down. Esperanza's pitifully shrunken body became visible.

A shiver tracked up Samantha's spine. Kneeling, she was about to brush away a thick lock of Esperanza's auburn hair when Diana stopped her.

"Peter and I should really process the body."

"Process the body?"

Peter kneeled beside her and said, "There may be evidence on her. A bit of debris or something else that will let us track down where they might have taken her."

She nodded and stepped away. Peter and Diana slowly and methodically collected evidence.

She looked across the room at Ryder, his arms crossed before him. A tight set to his features. He was clearly troubled, but whether it was about Esperanza or something else—like involving his people in her problem—she didn't know. Until he asked, "Who's going to process all these materials you're gathering?"

"I have a friend who has been running the prints for me," Peter said. "But we've hit a dead end since they lead to classified files."

Diana's head snapped up. "When did you find that out?"

"Just before Samantha called about Diego. I was about to phone you since—"

"If I didn't know Sloan was dead, I'd think this was his work," Ryder interjected.

Diana laid a hand on Ryder's chest. "*Amor,* Sloan isn't alive."

"Do we know that for sure? If we're wrong, he may turn his attention to Melissa."

Samantha followed his gaze. Sebastian eased an arm around Melissa's waist and then downward to rest along the soft swell of Melissa's abdomen.

It was like a kick to her gut. Melissa was pregnant. "What are you thinking, Ryder? A mortal keeper who's married? Having children? Do you care nothing for her?"

A low and angry sound was the only warning of Ryder's transformation. Diana blocked his way, much as she had so many days before. "All of my keepers have had families," he said. "How could I presume to rob them of a normal life? It's funny you should ask me this. You care so little—"

"Care so little?" she said as tears came to her eyes. "I have no keeper, Ryder. I don't want to burden anyone in my life with such a charge. Nor would I claim to love someone and force them to live a life that would bring them nothing but sadness."

Her words must have cut him deeply. His transformation quickly fled and his dark eyes swept down to his lover, filled with apology. Filled with so much love, it was painful to behold.

Samantha turned away and met Peter's gaze. Pain, so strong it was almost a blow, hit her once more at what she saw in his eyes. The remnants of whatever Peter might have felt for her had been driven from him with her words. All warmth left his hazel-green eyes; they turned cold, hard and unyielding as he said, "This bickering will accomplish nothing, but

Samantha is right. We need to keep Melissa's involvement to a minimum and we need to keep a close eye on her."

Diana, who had been facing Ryder, turned to the two of them. "I'll make sure Sebastian stays close. Plus, I think she should take a few days off from the hospital until we can get more info."

"How will we get more info?" Peter questioned. "I couldn't access those classified files."

"Sebastian could hack in, but I'd rather not have to resort to that. My partner, David, helped with that before. As for the physical evidence we have here…" She paused and shot an uneasy glance at Ryder. "Maggie Gonzalez can help with the forensics."

It didn't take a rocket scientist to realize what Ryder was thinking. Even more people involved in Samantha's problem. *Her problem.* "I appreciate all that you've done, but I think it's time I took care of this myself. Just by myself."

With that, she walked out of the room.

Chapter 23

Peter chased after her, although he didn't really have a clue what to say. Except maybe what he'd already said. "You can't do this alone, Samantha."

She shook her head. "Peter, I've been going it alone for almost one hundred and forty years."

"That's what you might want to tell yourself, but you haven't. You had Ryder—"

"Who I sired."

"And Diego—"

"Who's now missing."

"And all those women and children who need you," he finished, even though there was one more thing niggling in his brain, waiting to be said. Although after what she said to Ryder, Peter doubted that she wanted to hear it. Plus, he doubted his own conviction. Despite his best efforts, he was still stuck on Con number one.

Samantha examined him carefully and as if sensing his indecision, she took advantage of it like the hunter she was. Uncaring of the two people who stood watching, she morphed. Her eyes glowing with that weird light and her fangs protruding far below the line of her upper lip, she stepped toward him and cupped his cheek. Leaning forward, she nuzzled his nose with hers and brushed his lips with hers. Her voice deeper, and with that odd animal tinge, she said, "And what about you? Do I have you now, Peter? The way I am?"

It took all of his strength not to pull away or flinch as she brought her lips to his. He reminded himself that this was Samantha, the woman he'd cared about. A woman he'd kissed with affection. Her skin was warm and smooth. More human. And he wanted to restore that human and drive away the vampire she was using to scare him off.

He moved his thumb along the edge of her mouth as she opened it against his. Her fang nipped his lip, drawing blood. She pulled away and met his gaze.

He didn't waver in his determination to fight the beast she had set loose. With his thumb, he traced the edges of her lips and then boldly ran his finger down the long, bright white surface of one fang. "Do you think this will scare me away from doing what's right?"

"What's right? Tell me what's right about this undead life, Peter?"

He grabbed her arm and pulled. A mistake.

"Don't touch me," she roared and with a swipe of her arm, sent him flying across the room.

He crashed into the far wall, his shoulder connecting forcefully as he broke through the Sheetrock. His other arm ached just as much from the shock of her blow.

Simon grew agitated again at Samantha's display of violence. His pitiful wails filled the room and she quickly became human and rushed to his side, trying to calm the old keeper.

Melissa, Sebastian and Diana hurried to Peter's aid.

"Are you okay, Peter?" Diana asked and laid a hand on his shoulder. The one that didn't feel like it was broken, just bruised. He rubbed at the other shoulder and winced at the pain, not to mention the numbness, that ran down his arm.

"Let me look at that," Melissa probed at his arm.

He grimaced at her touch and cursed beneath his breath.

"It's dislocated, Peter. We'll have to pop it back into place," Melissa said.

Peter glanced across the length of the room to where Samantha sat by Simon. At Melissa's words, she clapped a hand over her mouth, obviously distressed at what she had done. Funny thing was, he wanted to go and comfort her, tell her he understood why she had reacted as she had, but she didn't give him the chance.

She raced out of the apartment.

"Great. Another vamp out there ready to be grabbed," Peter said.

Diana shot a glance at Ryder and he gave her a shocked look. "You want *me* to go after her?"

"*Por favor.* Just keep an eye on her. She's scared and unsure of what to do." Diana laid a hand over Ryder's heart as if to remind him he had one.

Ryder gritted his teeth. "Darlin', you sure know how to make life difficult."

"*Por favor.* For me."

"A low, but effective blow," he said and with a quick parting kiss, went after Samantha.

Once Ryder left, Diana gave Peter a pained look. "This is going to hurt."

Peter shrugged, then cursed at the extreme discomfort in his injured shoulder. After a few deep breaths to tamp down the pain, he said, "Do you think it'll hurt more than finding out she's a vamp?"

Diana looked from Melissa to Sebastian. "Let's get his arm fixed. After, I'd like you to take Simon and get him settled at Ryder's. Lock up and don't go anywhere."

"And what do you plan on doing?" Sebastian asked his sister.

"I'll drive Peter home and then meet you at Ryder's apartment."

Melissa probed at Peter's arm again and told Sebastian, "Hold him steady while I pull his arm back into the socket."

"Let me," Diana said and wrapped her arms around Peter. "On three."

"One," Melissa said, but Peter chose to think about something other than the pain that would shortly follow.

"You know a year ago—" he began.

"Two."

"I would have loved to have you hold me," he said and met Diana's concerned gaze.

"Three," Melissa said. Beside him, Diana braced him tightly while Melissa yanked.

Pain reverberated along the length of his arm, weakening his knees until with an odd pop, his shoulder wrenched back into place. His breath rough, he said, "Thanks."

Melissa nodded. "Let me get you a sling and something for the tenderness and inflammation."

"You okay, dude?" Sebastian asked.

Although it seemed like every bone in his body was broken, he nodded and said, "I'll be fine. Keep a close eye on Melissa."

Sebastian peered across the room to where his wife rummaged through her medical bag. "I won't let her out of my sight."

Melissa helped Peter with the sling and handed Diana some medication. "Ice your shoulder when you get home."

Peter nodded and with Diana's assistance, walked to the sofa. He sat down on its arm while Melissa and Sebastian rounded up a few things and left with Simon.

Diana asked, "Are you ready to go?"

His legs were a little stronger and he nodded. "About as ready as I'll ever be."

He was only a bit wobbly as he rose, but he waved off Diana's assistance. Together they went down to Diana's car and drove to Peter's apartment.

They were silent for the longest time until Diana finally asked, "Did you mean what you said before? About you know, the whole 'holding me' part, because—"

"You're not interested. I knew that," he said, trying to clear the air.

"That's good because Ryder and me are…"

She hesitated and that delay puzzled him. "Ryder and you are what?"

"Lovers. Friends," she answered quickly, but her hands tightened on the steering wheel.

Behind her words, her tone was uneasy, so he had to ask, "But not living with one another? Unless I heard wrong, you said, 'Ryder's apartment.'"

She shrugged as she pulled into a spot in front of his building, but she didn't face him. "We don't live together. Not yet anyway. Maybe not ever."

Her words surprised him. The emotions he'd seen pass between his friend and Ryder were intense. Then Samantha's words came back to him. "I'm sorry, Diana. I didn't mean to upset you."

She gave a harsh laugh. "You tell yourself you can deal with not having a normal life. With always being in the dark, especially when that time in the dark makes you feel more alive than you ever have in your entire life."

Peter searched her face and noted the glint of tears in her eyes. "But?"

"Something like this happens. Something to remind you that no matter how you might delude yourself into thinking your life isn't all that far from normal…"

She couldn't finish. She just dragged in a rough breath. They sat there together in the car until she had recovered.

He examined her face one last time. "Are you okay?"

Diana nodded. "I noticed some surveillance cameras at Diego's place. I'm going to head back and see if the tapes will help us. In the morning, I'll get David and Maggie working on whatever evidence we have."

She was back to being the Diana he knew, competent and in control. But he'd seen the woman beneath—the insecure one she didn't let many see. "I appreciate our talk. I'm confused about things and knowing I'm not alone—"

"Helps a lot. I'm glad we talked, too, Peter." She gave him a forceful hug, although he couldn't control the flinch from the pain that came to his shoulder. Diana motioned to his injury. "Take some medicine and ice up that shoulder. It should feel better in a few days."

He chuckled and said, "A few days, huh? I guess I should look at the upside."

Diana shot him a quizzical look and he added, "It makes me forget the pain in my neck from Foley nearly strangling me the other night."

She laughed as he'd intended and he got out of her car.

As he was slipping his key into the lock of his building, the sense that he was not alone made him pause. Looking upward, he searched the rooftops and fire escapes, but saw nothing in the murky light of late dusk.

With a painful shrug, he went inside.

Chapter 24

Samantha wasn't alone.

She had perceived a presence and power chasing her during her headlong flight from Diego's apartment.

She'd arrived at the building across from Peter's in time to see him at his door while Diana drove away. When Peter seemed to sense her, she'd stepped back, right into Ryder.

"What are you doing here?"

With a confused shake of his head, he shifted away from her. "Quite frankly, I don't know."

"You don't know? Did Diana tell you to follow me?"

Ryder crossed his arms and calmly answered, "Yes."

Because she was hurt and angry and confused, she said, "And like a good dog, you do everything she tells you?"

He moved then. Quickly. She found herself dangling inches off the ground. Ryder had her throat in a painful grasp.

She kicked him square in the stomach, weakening his grip

enough that she could escape. She prepared for him to try and contain her again, but he just straightened and rubbed at a spot on his midsection. "Why does it upset you so? My relationship with Diana?"

"We're not supposed to mix with them."

He laughed, surprising her. "Really? Is that written in a book somewhere. *Undead for Dummies?*" Before she could reply, he continued, "Even if there is such a rule, who's going to stop me? Or you for that matter?"

"Me?" she said. "What makes you think—"

"That you love him? You can try to push him away, but he doesn't strike me as the kind who'll run from what he wants."

Samantha walked to the ledge of the building, considering what Ryder had said. Across the way, the lights in Peter's apartment were on. A shadow passed by the window before the lights went off in one room and snapped to life in another.

Ryder joined her. "It's not easy on them. They're always conflicted about the whole bloodsucker thing and what happens when they grow old and wrinkled."

"And you're not?"

A rough sigh escaped his lips. "I die a little every day knowing it's one less day with her. Knowing that I could lose control of the demon and hurt her."

Samantha understood the feeling. "Would you turn her? Or prolong her life like a keeper's?"

He shook his head. "I wasn't aware of the whole keeper thing."

"I know you don't like being what you are, but it's not fair to her if you don't know what you're capable of." She met his troubled gaze.

"I've told myself that a thousand times," he said. "Only…I need someone to show me."

"I understand." She stared down at Peter's apartment. "And I need someone to convince me—"

"To go down there? Apologize for bruising the boy a bit?" His joke lightened the mood, as if he sensed how much guilt she felt about what she had done earlier.

She smiled as he had intended, but it quickly fled when she remembered what had happened last time she'd crossed a line with Peter. "I'm not sure I can control myself. The demon—"

He held a hand up to stop her. "You'll know what to do, Samantha. As for the demon, who says humans don't like a little bite in their life?"

His words surprised her, as did his abrupt departure. He jumped to the next rooftop and leaped from one building to the next, heading uptown.

She stood there until she could no longer see Ryder, then she once again stared at Peter's apartment. The lights in his bedroom were off and at the window, a bit of pink fluttered in and out of the opening with a passing breeze.

It was like a flag calling her to come down. Look inside. See him in his bed.

Heat snaked through her as she recalled watching him the other night. As she remembered kissing him, while she was in her vampire state. She'd nipped his lip and a droplet of his blood, warm and filled with life, had marked his skin before he'd licked it away.

She imagined licking it. Licking him. Kissing him. Making love with him.

She had to know, had to try. Because even if taking it further meant dying a little every day, she preferred that kind of death to never being alive.

To never knowing any kind of love.

With that thought, she stepped back from the ledge and made the leap.

Peter didn't know what woke him.

He'd fallen asleep almost immediately after taking the pain medicine Melissa had given him. It had made him a bit woozy, with a medicinal kind of happy buzz, but now, he was fully alert and aware. Rising, he propped one arm on the bed and gazed toward the open window. That was when he saw a shadow out on the fire escape. *Her shadow.*

Why hadn't she come in? Was it because vampires couldn't enter unless invited? She could sit out on that ledge all night long if he wanted her to.

But he wanted her in here with him.

He wanted to settle things between them once and for all.

"Come in, Samantha," he called out.

She raised the window and slipped into his room.

Peter snapped on the light so he could see her better. She stood by the window, looking uncertain in her faded figure-hugging jeans and a black cashmere sweater that enhanced her coloring. She looked normal, desirable, despite the fact that she'd basically kicked his ass.

"To what do I owe the pleasure of this visit?" He sat up in bed and winced from the twinge in his shoulder. She was immediately at his side, a worried look on her face.

"I'm sorry I hurt you. I didn't mean to, only—"

"You don't like being touched," he finished for her, knowing full well the reason for her reaction.

"I shouldn't have used my vamp power, but around you…I can't control my emotions." A becoming blush came to her pale cheeks. He had the answer to his question about how she would look when she blushed. *Even more beautiful.*

"Normally I'd say that's a good thing, but the pain in my shoulder says otherwise." He wasn't quite sure why he teased her. Teasing was a man-woman thing. A prelude to deepening a connection. But she wasn't human and he was totally uncertain about his attraction to her—except knowing she was a vampire had done little to dim his fascination.

She clasped and unclasped her hands nervously as she stood by his bed. "I'm sorry. I just wanted you to know that."

The need to comfort her arose again, sharp and demanding. Almost unconsciously, he laid a hand over hers. "Samantha, it's okay. I understand."

She shook her head and the long waves of her hair shifted with the vehemence of her movement. "I don't think you really do."

Asserting gentle pressure, he pulled her beside him on the bed. The turmoil in her eyes was difficult to see, but also encouraging. It meant she was as conflicted as he was. That she was maybe thinking about their seemingly impossible relationship and wishing that it wasn't so impossible.

Armed with that, he brushed away a long lock of hair, and urged her to meet his gaze. "Tell me. Help me understand."

Samantha examined his features, from the shaggy sun-bleached hair to his hazel-green eyes, shining brightly with an emotion she wished was hope. She gave in to her desire and brushed back a lock of his hair. As silken and alive beneath her fingers as she remembered. It made her smile before reality jolted her. She pulled her hand back.

"Samantha?" He rubbed his thumb along her cheek.

She pressed into that caress like a cat needing attention. "You make me feel...alive," she finally said.

He continued to stroke her face, running the back of his hand along the line of her jaw. "After my wife...I didn't think I'd ever want a relationship again."

"My husband was no prize package either," she said and the smile that had been on his face grew grim.

"I know he hurt you. But not all men hurt."

She nodded. "I know. Now. I know you won't mean to hurt me—"

"But you think I will?" he asked. "And you think you'll hurt me, too, don't you?"

With a shrug, she said, "It's inevitable. You're human and I'm—"

"A beautiful woman, although I won't hold that against you. But I would like to hold you, even though that seems crazy. Can we start that way? Just holding? Until we both figure out what we want?" His voice was expectant, boyishly trusting. It was that Boy Scout sincerity that lessened her resistance. With a nod, she moved until she was sitting beside him, his good arm wrapped around her shoulder, pulling her tight into his side.

They were quiet as they sat there, his body warming hers. His gentle strength and easy nature calming her disquiet. "This is nice," she finally said.

"I could get used to this." He dropped a kiss on her forehead.

She laid her hand on his chest. His heartbeat was strong. True. Painful since her own heart was an iffy thing in so many ways. "This isn't a good idea, Peter."

But up close, there was no denying the need in his gaze. Impossible to resist the temptation to nuzzle her nose against the warmth of his skin.

The rasp of his evening beard was a sharp contrast to the smoothness of his lips as he moved them against her cheek, trailed them closer and closer to her mouth until she met his lips with her own.

They were so warm. Wet as he deepened the kiss.

Whatever it took, she was going to allow herself this one night. This one chance to feel alive.

She opened her mouth against his, sampled the vitality of his human breath. The dampness of his tongue as she caressed it with her own.

He broke away from her, his breathing rough and his cheeks flushed. "I don't want to stop."

"Neither do I only…I'm not sure I can control myself, Peter," she admitted, suddenly aware of the heat gathering in the pit of her stomach. Human desire that might become vampire lust.

He grinned, a boyishly sexy grin and said, "I'm not sure I can either since…" He glanced down at the sheet and she tracked his gaze to the juncture of his legs where it was clear nothing was happening yet. "Melissa gave me some medicine and… Shit."

She kissed him, while whispering against his lips, "I just want to spend time with you tonight, love. Have you hold me."

He smiled. "Anything you want, Samantha. Anything."

His words and tone made her shift back for a second. "Anything?"

He raised his hand and brushed back a lock of her long hair. "If you can't control it… We can stop, Samantha. I won't press you for more than you want because…I'm still not sure what I want either."

A shudder racked her and it took all of her strength to suppress the demon from emerging, wakened by the power of the emotions he roused within her.

"Samantha?"

She met his gaze. "I want the woman in me to be loved, Peter. She's never known what it is to be loved."

She closed her eyes tight against tears, but they escaped

from beneath her lids anyway. He wiped them away. "You talk of the woman as if she's not you, Samantha."

"It's been so long, she doesn't seem real to me anymore."

He ran his fingers through her hair, his caress gentle. "She's still there, Samantha. And maybe tonight she'll be real again."

"How can you be so sure?"

He kissed her deeply. "I'm not sure of anything anymore. You've taken everything I've ever believed and tossed it on its head."

"So why are you still here?" she asked, unsure of where this road would lead them.

His grin was broad and lit up his face, making her think of sunny days and a summer beach. "Because I can't imagine not taking a chance right now. Can you?"

Chapter 25

Then Peter kissed her, a slow enticing kiss meant to show her just how much he wanted her. He caressed her lips with his, a second before kissing the small scar she worried when she was upset.

He realized then, there were other scars that needed to be healed as well, both physical and mental. Even without the side effects of the pain medication—not to mention the ache in his shoulder—it was clear that tonight was meant to be taken slowly.

Patiently, he explored the sensitive hollow where her neck and shoulder joined, easing aside the collar of the black cashmere sweater so he could taste her skin. She moaned and held him close, and he slid his hand beneath the hem, caressing her skin all the way to her breasts.

Moving back up to her mouth, he was kissing her as he finally cupped her breast, stroking the hard tip of it beneath the satiny fabric of her bra. She expelled a rough sigh and a moan.

He said against her lips, "I want to kiss you there."

A shudder ripped through her. Her blue eyes were dark with passion, her pupils wide and dilated. No glow. These were her human eyes locked with his. Her human lips, swollen and wet from his kisses.

"I'd like that," she answered.

With her permission granted, they both reached for the hem of her sweater at the same time, their hands fumbling before he opted for placing his at her waist and watching instead. Black cashmere drifted upward, revealing the smooth creaminess of the skin at her waist and then her stomach. Moved ever upward past her ribs and finally over her head to reveal her breasts in a black satin bra, trimmed with black lace.

The color was a sharp contrast to her pale skin. To the deep golden color of his hand, tanned from years in the sun.

She watched as he caressed her, and as he grasped the tip between his thumb and forefinger, she gave the barest hint of a gasp. He shot a quick glance at her face. The tiniest of blushes blossomed along her cheeks.

Bolstered by her shy smile, he undid the front clasp of her bra. Her breasts spilled free, generous in their proportion given that she was slender elsewhere. Full and firm, with large caramel-colored nipples that he could no longer resist. He took one into his mouth while he pleasured the other tip with his fingers.

Samantha couldn't contain the moan he pulled from her as he made love to her breasts. The movements of his fingers and mouth were sure, but tender. She cradled his head to her, loving the way his longish hair swept across her skin.

Marveling at the wonderful color of his skin, rich and healthy against her fairer tones.

Mon dieu, the warmth of him. Of his skin everywhere it touched hers. Alive. Welcoming her into his human world.

She pressed herself closer, needing the life that poured off him in waves. But it wasn't enough as the barrier of her jeans kept her from feeling all of him.

"Peter." Together they worked at baring all of her, the jeans coming off in a flash and flying across the room to land in a heap of denim.

She was naked.

He groaned at the sight of her fully revealed to him and rubbed the back of his hand against the dark curls at the juncture of her thighs.

She needed to touch him too. She moved her hand between his legs, intrigued by his dark blond curl. "You're a real blonde," she teased.

He chuckled. "I am and you're…God, you're so beautiful."

It had been so long—maybe never—that a man had told her she was beautiful. But she was coming to realize Peter wasn't like any other man she had ever met.

"You're beautiful, too." She ran her hand up his body to the muscles of his chest, where she idly drew her thumb across his dark copper nipple. It beaded beneath her fingers. "Do you like?"

"Hmm," he answered in a lazy tone. "I like you touching me. Wherever. And you?" he asked as he mimicked her motions, running his thumb along the turgid tip of her breast. His nose brushed hers, playfully nuzzling her before he brushed the lightest of kisses along her lips. "Tell me what else you like."

A little uncertain, she teased, "Why, Detective. You like to talk?"

The grin that lit up his face was devilishly naughty. "Definitely. I want you to tell me what you want next, Samantha."

She sucked in a breath as she imagined just what she

wanted next. Almost without thinking, she blurted out, "I want you to kiss me again. Where your hand is."

Peter didn't hesitate, lowering his head and kissing the tip of her, just once before murmuring against her breast, "And now?"

Samantha tangled her fingers through his marvelous hair. "Kiss me again…and again."

And he did, nibbling and suckling until her body was shaking with need. Until she was clenching her thighs together to battle the emptiness inside her. She cried out his name as one forceful tug nearly sent her over the edge.

"May I touch you…here?" His hand was at the juncture of her thighs. She answered him by raising one leg and letting him ease his leg between hers.

She swallowed her shocked gasp at his touch.

"You're so warm. So wet."

She hadn't realized it until now, but she had been growing warmer with his lovemaking. Unlike the other night, so far the human remained in control. She gripped his shoulders, her grasp on him tightening as the sure movement of his hand between her legs brought her closer and closer to the edge. As the heat inside her increased, the first stirring of the beast came. It smelled her arousal and the scent of his flesh. The singing of the blood in his veins.

Shaking her head, she called out his name, almost in fear. "Peter."

Her tone made him raise his head from her breast. It was her eyes he noted first. The blue was disappearing as the light of the vampire grew. Her breathing was rough and unsteady as he stroked her to completion. But she was afraid of that completion. Of the human release that might free the demon within.

He wanted to temper that fear. Keep the woman with him.

Kissing her, he said, "She's still there, Samantha. Real and wanting to feel this. Hold on to your true self and control the beast."

Her body shuddered against his and she closed her eyes, bit her lower lip.

He leaned close, licked the spot she was worrying with her teeth, opened his mouth against hers until she responded to his kiss.

"Peter, I…I want you—" She couldn't finish. A moan escaped her lips as he slipped yet another finger inside her. Her body responded, pulling at him. Moving against his hand as her climax neared.

"Tell me what you want now, Samantha."

She opened her eyes once more. The glow was gone and only the crystalline blue of her human eyes was visible. "Kiss me. Down there," she rasped, her breathing uneven.

A shiver worked through his body as he imagined loving her with his mouth. Between his legs, the first stirring of life finally came. With each slow kiss, he moved downward, taking his time while he paused to lick and suck and trail a line of kisses down the center of her.

He slipped between her thighs. With a quick glance at her face, he nuzzled the curls with his nose before he tongued the center of her.

She arched off the bed at the first touch of his mouth. He tried to soothe her, running the back of his hand along her nether lips as he said, "Ssh, love. We'll take this slow."

Murmuring something almost unintelligible, she grasped his shoulders and urged him closer.

He answered her petition, bringing his mouth to the center of her, where he ran his tongue over the hard bud nestled beneath her curls. He eased first one finger and then another into her, slowly stoking her passion while he sucked at her clitoris. Bit at it gently. Fighting his own growing need so that she could reach her completion.

The muscles of his shoulders were hard beneath her hands. As he kissed and sucked and bit, moved within her, she arched her back, pressed her hips upward, seeking what she had been denied for over a century.

His loving and her human response to it.

A woman's cry of need and completion and devotion.

Her desire was growing, rising inside of her, but along with it was the beast, tasting the salt of his skin. Smelling the scents of arousal as she climbed higher and higher.

"Peter, please," she pleaded as she struggled to contain the demon.

He must have sensed how close to the edge she was, for he slowly shifted his body upward until he was lying between her legs. He was magnificently hard now and poised at her entrance.

At his delay, she met his gaze. That wonderful hazel-green gaze that invited her to step into his world. To become woman to his man. He smiled then, that devastatingly boyish grin, urging her to play.

Almost without volition, she found herself smiling back.

"Are you ready to be mine? To let me know the woman you are?"

The intensity of his gaze and words nearly undid her, but with them came fear. "My undead life, Peter? Is that what you truly want?"

"I want you," he responded, but he didn't wait for her reply to thrust inside.

The feel of him stole her breath and her heart. There was no turning back she realized as he began to move, drawing her with him into a world of emotions she hadn't ever expected to experience.

While he moved, he kissed her.

She could taste herself on his lips and in turn, wanted to taste him.

She licked his neck and the hollow of his shoulder. She licked him again and this time, opened her mouth and sucked the saltiness of his skin. He moaned.

She rolled until he was beneath her. The position buried him deep inside and she paused for a moment, absorbing the sensation of her body accommodating his breadth and length. Of his heat tucked tight within.

As she moved slowly on him, heat grew. For a moment she feared the demon inside would rise up, but it didn't because the human in her wanted him too much. She desired the mortal release swelling over her body more than the satisfaction that would come from feeding on him.

She shifted her hips, driving him in and out as she reached for her climax. He guided her, his hands on her hips, urging her on until she barely had the strength to continue.

Sensing she was tiring, Peter exerted gentle pressure and rolled her beneath him. His own body was slick with sweat. His breathing rough and labored. He was near completion, but he wanted to gift her with her release first. Slipping in and out of her, he made his strokes more determined and caressed her clitoris with his thumb until she cried out his name and arched off the bed.

He stilled then, giving her a moment to come down a bit. He was still rock hard, still ready to bring her to yet another climax, which he did, more slowly this time.

It was only after his own harsh cry echoed hers that he allowed himself to drop beside her and spoon against her back. He wrapped his arms around her waist, holding her close.

"That was nice," he said.

She laid her hands on his forearms and sleepily teased, "Just nice?"

He smiled and tucked her close. "Can you stay the night?"

She chuckled. "Only if you promise me one thing."

There was a playful tone in her words and so he went along with it. "Only one? I was kind of hoping for more than one."

Her laugh this time was broader and she turned in his arms to face him. She surprised him by reaching down and stroking him.

He surprised himself by instantly responding, immediately growing hard as she slipped her hand up and down his shaft. "Um, Samantha? Is that the one thing you wanted?"

"Not really," she said and moved downward, kissing her way along his body until her lips were just above the tip of him. "I think it was this," she said and took him into her mouth.

Chapter 26

His dislocated shoulder was stiff and achy.

His legs and arms were sore.

His penis... He reached down to make sure it was still there, and yes, there it was, slightly tender, but amazingly, growing hard once more.

With her back toward him, Samantha was still in bed at nearly five in the morning.

She kept a human schedule, so he suspected she wouldn't be trapped in his apartment if they tarried a little. But when he recalled the whirlwind of activity that was the shelter in the morning, he knew he should see if she needed to go.

He laid a hand on her shoulder and gave her a light shake.

She murmured, "Can't go right now."

He rose on one elbow and glanced at the window, where only the barest hint of dawn streaked the morning sky. "Will the sun be too strong later?"

She turned toward him, a sleepy look on her face. "Not in the early morning. I'm just a bit tired, although I should get back to the shelter before they get worried."

"Probably." He shifted until he was lying close to her, his erection hard against the soft skin of her belly.

Her eyes opened wide. "Are you sure you're not the vamp? Your…staying power seems—"

"Superhuman. Maybe it's the company, love," he answered honestly, since he couldn't remember ever being this hot for anyone before.

She smiled and kissed him. Against his lips, she said, "Even as tired as I am, it seems a shame not to take advantage of this before reality intrudes."

He couldn't argue. Mindful that both of them were feeling the effects of a very long and traumatic night, he opted for something slower and infinitely more tender than their earlier lovemaking.

Easing her thigh over his, he shifted until he joined with her and simply stayed within while he caressed her breasts and kissed her.

Her breath hitched with the way he slowly stretched her as he entered. She nearly came right then, but managed to control herself so she could savor the growing passion. He fingered her breasts and made love to her mouth, which caused her to pull and clench around him with her need.

When she would have moved on him, he gently urged her to be still. "Easy, love. It'll happen."

He kept his actions tender so the demon would not rouse. And then it finally happened. A slow swell of pleasure rolled over her, bringing fulfillment different from the wild rushing waves of the night before.

Through both, she'd stayed human. With his gentleness and

encouragement, she'd experienced his loving like a normal woman. Like she never had before this.

She kissed him and he cradled her close so they could savor the last vestiges of their passion.

"Ah, Samantha. I could stay here all day with you, but we both have too much to do."

She turned in his arms to stare out the windows where the sky was slowly brightening with the approach of morning. "I should go back."

"I just need to grab a quick shower and then I'll take you," he said and moved from her side.

She flipped in bed to face him once again, watching as he gathered what he would need for the day. "You don't need to. I can go back—"

He turned to her, his face serious. "I want to make sure you're safe. I'll take you back."

"But you should get more rest." He could use the sleep to recover from the injury to his shoulder.

Peter walked back to the bed and cupped her cheek. "I'm fine. Plus, I can grab a quick nap at the shelter before I head to work. That is, if you don't mind me in your bed."

Samantha smiled and covered his hand with hers. "The only thing I'll mind is not being there with you."

The Artemis Shelter was still quiet when she and Peter walked through the door. Everything seemed in order. Safe and secure.

She gave him a grateful smile. "Thanks for everything."

He laid a hand on her waist and kissed her. "Do you need help with anything?"

She shook her head. "No, I'm fine. Go get some rest. I'll wake you later."

As she watched him walk down to her room, she became aware of the presence of others and glanced up the stairs. Sofia was there, along with Leslie and another of the shelter's occupants, sitting on the steps and peeping through the railings. They were all grinning and clearly pleased.

"Is everything fine?" she asked, wondering why they were spying on her.

"Girl, if everything's fine with you, everything's fine with us," Sofia replied with a wink.

Samantha thought of Peter in her room. With a smile of her own, she replied, "It's never been better."

Which prompted a whoop from Sofia, who came down the steps and embraced her. The two other women quickly followed and Samantha found herself in the center of a rather boisterous and enthusiastic group hug.

"We're so happy for you. The detective seems like such a nice guy," Leslie said, and the other two women echoed that sentiment.

She was taken aback, never having really had female friends. Never having shared confidences or other girlfriend things. It brought tears to her eyes. "I'm happy, too."

After a few more hugs and kisses, she excused herself to begin the morning routine, putting on coffee and making breakfast. Preparing lunches for everyone. It was toward the end of breakfast when Peter came down to the kitchen.

Seeing him, a number of the kids raced over to welcome him.

It was like a homecoming. He seemed so happy surrounded by the kids. He was the kind of man who should have children of his own. Something she could never give him. First, because she was undead and she'd never heard of a human-vampire hybrid. Secondly, because even if it was remotely possible, Elias's beating had made her infertile.

He deserved a wife and kids. She bit her lip to fight back the tears.

Returning her attention to the plate of bacon and eggs she was preparing, she failed to hear him as he approached and laid a gentle hand on her shoulder.

"Penny for your thoughts," he said, leaning close and brushing a kiss along the side of her face.

"I'm not really sure you want to hear those thoughts." It might be best for them to reconsider the night they had just spent together.

He sighed deeply and squeezed her shoulder. "Not right now, Samantha. For right now, imagine that it might be possible."

"What?" she asked, playing dumb.

"The home. The kids. The happily ever after."

She hated that he could be so intuitive, but then again, he was a cop. Getting a read on people was a necessity in his line of work.

Turning to look at him over her shoulder, she held up the plate and said, "Biscuit?"

"Please." He took the dish from her hands and once again brushed a kiss along the side of her face. "Thank you."

She wouldn't ask what for, afraid of his answer. Afraid that she'd break down into tears with everyone watching them with interest.

Peter must have realized her fragile state since he didn't linger. Instead he returned to the table and let himself be engaged by the children's conversation.

Before she knew it, everyone was heading out, including Sofia, who said she was leaving early to study at the library. Which left Samantha and Peter, standing in the upstairs hallway awkwardly, wondering what to do next.

"I don't like the idea of you being alone here, but I need to get to work," he said, shooting a quick glance at his watch.

"If it'll make you feel better, I can head to Ricardo's," she offered.

"Ricardo, huh?" Peter shoved his hands into his pockets and jingled the change there.

It took her a second to realize he was jealous. "Ricardo is just a friend. Nothing else."

"He's a good-looking guy," Peter said.

She reached up, ran her hand across the blush of color in his cheeks. "He is handsome, don't you think?" she teased, but quickly added, "My interests, however, lie elsewhere. As do Ricardo's, I think."

His uncertainty fled. He twined his fingers with hers. "Really?"

Samantha nodded. "A young nurse whose mother Ricardo was trying to heal."

"Heal? Do you really—"

"Ricardo is truly gifted, Peter. It's how he sensed what I was. His interest in the nurse is the second reason why there can never be anything between us."

"Second reason?" he asked. "And what's the first?"

"Silly boy." She raised on her tiptoes and brushed a kiss on his lips. "You're reason number one."

Against her lips, she felt him smile. After a long and intense kiss, he said, "I'll walk you down."

"I'd appreciate that."

Chapter 27

Blake held Meghan close, trying to offer comfort as Diego's screams pierced the quiet of the early morning. Her body shuddered with each scream. Eventually, Diego grew silent, which only seemed to upset her more.

"It'll be okay," Blake said and rubbed her naked back in an effort to reassure her.

"I didn't think they'd be able to capture him," she said softly.

He pulled away to look down at her. "You told them where to find him?"

Meghan's large green eyes swam with tears. "I was sure Diego could help us. That he'd be able to get away from them and find out where we were."

"Shit." Blake shook his head, imagining Diego's wrath. First, Blake had betrayed him by naming Esperanza and Samantha in the hopes that Diego would act to find them. And now Meghan's betrayal.

If the old professor didn't kill them all, there was no question in Blake's mind that Diego would seek vengeance. But he wouldn't let Diego hurt Meghan, no matter what it took.

"Good morning," said the old professor, his tone unctuous and triumphant. "Your friend is magnificent."

The professor's normally tidy person was marred by flecks of blood on his white shirt and tweed vest. Behind him, looking a little pale and bearing a Taser, was one of his goons. The bigger man's jeans and khaki T-shirt were also splattered with blood, but there was a lot more of it.

They'd obviously inflicted a lot of damage on Diego. If he was that badly injured, the likelihood of them getting free…

"What do you want?" Blake shouted from his corner of the cell.

"Why you two, of course. Your friend needs a little sustenance," the sick old man said.

Meghan grew more agitated. He tried his best to calm her. "Sshh, Megs. Don't worry."

"Oh, but she should. Diego said he'd drain her dry for betraying him." The professor turned to his assistant. "Bind them and bring them into the other cell."

"No," Meghan wailed, pulling out of his arms and racing to the opposite side of the cell.

The assistant fired the Taser at her first.

As her body jerked and shook, Blake ripped the electrodes from her body. She was slack when she fell into his arms.

"There's no need for that," he called out, rocking her like a baby.

The old man seemed to recognize the truth of Blake's words. Holding his hand out to his assistant, he snapped his fingers. "The manacles."

The assistant handed them to the professor, who then tossed them to Blake. "Chain her. Then come here to be bound."

Blake picked up the hardened steel chain and cuffs, and gently eased them over Meghan's wrists. There were still bruises from the last time she'd been cuffed, a testament to the fact that she was still not up to full strength, even with the blood bags the professor had provided.

After she was chained, he gently laid her on the ground, walked over to the bars of the cell and held his hands out to be cuffed. A few bruises marked his wrists as well, which worried him. In any state other than the height of his strength, he doubted he could defend himself and Meghan against Diego.

Diego was just too strong. But if the blood on the two humans was a sign, Diego might be badly injured.

Which brought relief, and despair.

They had both hoped Diego would save them.

But Samantha was still free. She might be able to find a way to help.

He flinched as the cuffs were locked around his wrists and the assistant, apparently just because he could, gave him a small zap with the cattle prod. The charge was enough to weaken Blake's knees. He had to grab the bars of the cell to keep from falling down.

The assistant smiled and was about to do it again when the professor restrained him. "Enough. We need him to carry the female into the other room."

"This one's cocky. I don't trust him not to try anything," he replied, but did as the old man asked.

Blake took in a deep breath or two, summoning all his strength to walk back to where Meghan lay huddled on the ground. But as he reached for her, she feebly pushed herself into the corner, shaking and crying.

"He'll kill me, Blake. He'll kill me," she repeated over and over.

He laid a hand on her shoulder. "He won't. Trust me. I'll protect you."

"How touching," the old man said cynically and clapped, as distant to their emotions as if he was watching a movie or a television show.

Blake wanted to lash out at him, but he'd learned quickly that it would accomplish nothing. So he picked up Meghan. She didn't fight him. Instead, she grabbed hold of his shoulders and laid her head on his naked chest.

Her grip was weak. If Diego did attack her...

He forced such thoughts from his mind and carried her to the door of the cell. It opened as he neared and the two men stepped to the side to allow him to walk into the large adjacent room where they had first tortured him and Meghan.

Blake could not have imagined what awaited them.

Diego was not chained to the hooks in the cement wall mainly because there weren't any hooks in the wall anymore. He was lashed with several chains to a large support beam in the center of the room. His head hung down loosely. There were an assortment of marks on his body, but no blood.

A few feet away, where the hooks used to be, lay the body of the professor's other assistant, his throat ripped out. There was a puddle of blood on the floor and Blake's stomach rumbled in hunger.

The old man must have heard since he said, "Go ahead, my boy. Feed yourself. Feed your little friend and of course, Diego. He'll need a little something for what I have planned."

With those words and a shove, the two men locked the door of the room.

At the sound, Diego finally roused. Slowly he picked up

his head. His eyes began to glow brightly as he said, "Blake. You're a dead man."

Peter shook hands with David Harris, Diana's partner, who then introduced Maggie Gonzalez, a physician and sometime assistant forensic specialist for the FBI.

He had not met Maggie during the course of either the Williams investigation or the more recent problems with Melissa Danvers. He would remember if he had. She was a stunning woman. Tall and auburn-haired with a slim athletic build. Her face was classically beautiful and yet, she didn't move him in the way that Samantha did.

"It's nice to finally meet you," Maggie said. "Diana speaks quite well of you."

"The same for you. I want to thank you for helping us."

David and Maggie sat down across from him at the conference room table and it was then Peter noticed the connection between them that they were obviously trying to ignore. He didn't have time to think on it further before Diana joined them.

"David. Were you able to get any information from your friend?" she asked.

"Actually, no, but by not getting information, I got information."

"Meaning?" Peter asked.

"My contact at the National Security Agency said that the heat has been on ever since Sloan was presumed dead. Apparently, the higher-ups don't look too kindly on ex-operatives dying under unusual circumstances, especially at one of their old safehouses."

"Which means?" Diana asked.

David clasped his hands together. "He wanted to know

why I needed information on two ex-agents who used to work with Sloan."

Peter was taken aback by what he was hearing. "The fingerprints belonged to ex-NSA agents?"

David nodded. "Not only ex-NSA, but on Sloan's team in 2003. They were working together to gather information on the possibility of a super-soldier unit. Like Sloan, they were terminated because the NSA believed they had become an unnecessary risk."

"And now they've become *our* unnecessary risk?" Peter jumped in with some exasperation. "This is one too many coincidences. The description of our culprit. Sloan's ex-colleagues involvement. The profile of the missing—"

"People," Diana said and shot him a warning look.

He'd been about to say vampires. The two agents sitting across from him had no clue as to the real reasons for their investigations.

"The evidence from the victim points to similarities between where she was taken and the area near the safehouse where Sloan was killed—" Maggie added.

"Presumably killed. The NSA isn't listing him as dead without a body," David corrected.

"Why does everything point back to Sloan?" Peter asked.

"David provided me with the information we had on Sloan. As sick as he was, it's unlikely he's still alive only…" Maggie paused and glanced at them uneasily. "The evidence you brought me included Sloan's fingerprint."

Diana laid her hands on the table and stared at her two friends. "If I'm hearing you both correctly, you think Sloan is still alive."

Maggie and David shot a look at one another before Maggie nodded. "Yes. I don't know how, but it seems possible. And, as I was saying, based on the evidence from the last victim, the culprit is taking them to a rural location. Near some woods. Probably with a lake or other body of water nearby."

"How do you know that?" Peter questioned.

"Minute traces of goose droppings as well as other detritus that would indicate she had been kept outside at some point. Everything combined is very similar to David's descriptions of where Sloan held Melissa Danvers hostage."

The chirping of Diana's phone broke the awkward silence that followed Maggie's pronouncement.

As Diana answered the phone, Peter addressed David and Maggie. "You two seem certain Sloan's involved in this."

"Add the evidence and the fingerprints to Sloan's missing body… It's too similar to Sloan's MO," Maggie said.

"Maybe Sloan's associates knew what he was doing and decided to copycat his activities," Peter offered up as an alternate explanation.

David shrugged. "That's possible, but I got the sense from my contact that Sloan's two associates were brawny, not brainy. Grabbing four or five people and barely leaving a clue is more in the brainy category."

Diana hung up, a worried look on her face. "Do you think you can get Samantha?" she asked Peter. "Melissa would like her opinion on something. Thank you, David, Maggie, for everything you've done."

Maggie gave Diana a hug. "Seems to me we just complicated things."

"No, I really appreciate your opinions," Diana answered before embracing her partner.

"Di, is there something else we should know about?" David asked in an uneasy voice.

Diana shot him a tight smile. "Not right now, David. But I appreciate all that you've done."

"Which means we should shut down any further inquiries?" Maggie asked.

Diana nodded. "For right now, we know all we need to know. If there's anything else, I'll be sure to warn you."

Although her friends accepted Diana's words, they were clearly uneasy. Peter considered it a testament to their trust in Diana that they didn't press any further.

After they left, she said, "We need to get Samantha over to Ryder's right away. Simon has grown very agitated. Melissa says his vital signs are fluctuating wildly. She's worried about him."

"Understood," he said.

Chapter 28

Meghan finished licking the last of the blood from her lips and watched as Blake fed Diego with the corpse of the old man's associate. The muscles of his shoulders and back bunched with the effort of lifting the dead man up so Diego could suck down what was left of his blood.

She'd taken a small bit for herself, both from the corpse and the blood that had spilled on the floor. Blake had taken none of it, declaring that the important thing was for her and Diego to strengthen themselves.

It had surprised her that he would make any effort to help Diego. After Diego's threat she would have fortified herself so she could defend herself against his attack.

Which was why she had greedily accepted the offer Blake made of first taste of the corpse and the blood on the floor. When Diego found out who had betrayed him to the old professor, he'd come after her. She needed to be ready to fight.

Funny thing really, this sudden urge to hang onto her undead life. Up until the kidnapping, she would have said that
she'd be more than happy to find a way out of her unnatural
existence. But since then…

Since Blake.

She observed him again. His arms were trembling from his
efforts since he wasn't at full strength. Rising, she went to his
assistance, easily lifting the corpse with the energy coursing
through her veins.

As she stood by Blake, she met Diego's gaze as he sucked
on the dead man's neck. Guilt made her turn away.

Diego fed for a few more minutes before he roughly
growled, "Enough."

She released her hold on the corpse. The suddenness of
bearing the weight forced Blake onto the ground beside it.

She kneeled down next to him. "I'm sorry, Blake."

He rose from his sprawl and cupped her cheek. "It's
okay, love."

"You're too weak. You need to feed so our fight will not
be over too quickly," Diego taunted from where he was lashed
to the beam.

Blake shook his head. "I won't fight you, Diego. I know I
shouldn't have given them Esperanza's or Samantha's names,
but I thought you would come for them…for us."

Meghan observed Diego's face as Blake's words registered. When Diego looked at her, she couldn't bear the condemnation in his eyes.

"It was you, little one? After all that we did for you?" he
said tightly, with the low ominous rumble of an oncoming
transformation.

Blake awkwardly got to his feet. "Do not waste your
strength, Diego. You will need all of it to escape."

Diego twisted against the chains holding him and plaster dust drifted down as the beam shifted slightly on its moorings. All three of them looked up.

"If the ceiling collapses, it may kill us all," Diego said.

"Better that than what the old psycho has planned," Meghan offered.

"Or what I have planned for you, little one."

"You'll have to go through me first." Blake laid a hand on her naked thigh to urge her to stand at his back.

"Ever the lovestruck fool, Blake. It'll get you killed, you know."

Blake shook his head and although he was facing Diego, he spoke to her. "There's a camera in the corner, Meghan. Take the shirt off the corpse and cover the lens."

Meghan did as he asked, wondering what he was up to. "Here's the deal, Diego. I help you get free and—"

"I promise not to kill you?" Diego laughed harshly. "Are you that much of a simpleton?"

"You're an honorable man, Diego. If you promise—"

"Did you see what Esperanza looked like? What they did to her?" His voice was haunted and filled with hurt.

"We tried to save her. To feed her, but she was already gone," Meghan tried to explain.

"She was always weak. She had a weak heart as a human and…" Diego gave a shrug of his broad shoulders and the chains binding him rattled with the movement.

"I'm sorry," Blake said. "We're sorry," he added on her behalf. He kneeled and worked at the belt on the dead man's waist. When he popped back up, he held a piece of the belt buckle.

"And your plan is?" Diego asked.

"I'm going to file this down and pick the lock on the chains, only we won't make a move—"

"Until they come back. Have at it then," he said, but Blake remained standing before him.

She took hold of his arm. "Blake? What's up?"

Blake shot a look at her, but returned his attention to Diego. "The deal is—I free you. I feed you. When you're free, you take Meghan with you. You promise not to hurt her."

Diego glanced from one to the other. As his gaze met hers, he must have seen something in her eyes. Something that told him leaving Blake behind would…

Although she could avoid Diego's scrutiny, it was impossible to ignore the pain in her heart. She gripped Blake's hand. "You don't need to do this. We can get out some other way."

Blake touched her cheek. "I'm sorry I turned you, Meghan. I want to make that up to you."

"Not this way, Blake. You don't need to do this," she whispered urgently.

"But I do, love," he said and kissed her. It was a gentle kiss, filled with longing and regret. It tugged at her heartstrings. As much as she had hated him for turning her, she thought she might hate him more now for leaving her.

"Deal," Diego said loudly, shattering the moment. "Just do it, *amigo*. The old bastard won't wait forever once he realizes he can't watch us."

Simon was calmer by the time Peter and Samantha arrived at Ryder's apartment.

Samantha sat beside him and laid her hand on the middle of his chest.

"They're hurting him. They're killing him," he said. Fear filled his voice.

"Don't worry, Simon. We will free Diego soon. Everything will be all right."

Simon nodded, closed his eyes and relaxed back into the pillows of the bed. Samantha motioned for Melissa to remain silent and follow her out of the room.

As soon as she had closed the door to the room where Simon was staying, Melissa asked, "Can you explain what's happening?"

"When a vampire makes a keeper—"

"It prolongs their life," Sebastian filled in for her based on their conversation of the night before.

"It does, but it also irrevocably binds that human to the vampire who made him. After a long time, the bond is so strong that what the vampire feels, the keeper feels. When the vampire dies—"

"The keeper dies." Melissa peered at Ryder. "Is that why you didn't prolong our lives?"

Ryder shook his head. "I didn't know about that aspect of being…" He hesitated and it was clear that even after more than a century, he still wasn't comfortable with what he was or what he could do.

Samantha glanced across the way at Peter. His gaze, was troubled and she could understand why. Immortality seemed like such a gift, unless you were the one who had to live it. Who had to watch everything around you change while you stayed the same. Who watched everyone around you die, while you lived day after interminable day.

"Clearly Diego is in trouble," Peter said to break the uncomfortable moment. "All we know is that Sloan may be alive—"

"Who's Sloan?" The others obviously had information they had yet to share with her.

"About two years ago, Ryder's keeper—Frederick Danvers—and his wife were murdered because of some journals Frederick kept," Diana explained.

Samantha was confused. "Journals about—"

"Me," Ryder interrupted. "About me and how he had apparently found something about my vampire cells that cured his terminally ill wife. His associate, Edward Sloan, was after the rest of the journals, trying to recreate the cure."

"For himself," Melissa said. "Sloan had cancer, but that wasn't what killed him. He took me hostage and he died in a fire caused during my rescue."

"And you're sure he's dead?"

"The fire that swept through the lab was so intense, it incinerated everything within the building, including his associate. Plus, after Sloan's death, we confirmed with his oncologist that at best, Sloan had only a few months left to live," Diana explained.

"Unless he was turned," Samantha said. "If he survived the fire and was turned—"

"But if he's a vampire why would he be after other vamps?" Sebastian asked.

At his question, Peter reached for his notes and read out loud from the pad. "No limp. Fifties at most. But our culprit's height, race and hair are the same. Not to mention the whole professor look."

"Sometimes when you're sired, you appear younger."

Diana nodded. "It's worth exploring since we have so few leads, only… Why would Sloan want Meghan?"

"And why would Meghan go with him?" Samantha asked, but it wasn't really a question. "Although if this…Sloan was able to find out about Frederick Danvers's cure for human illness—"

"Then maybe he's discovered how to heal without becoming a vampire." Diana looked over at Ryder. "Or how to reverse vampirism."

It was clear what both were thinking. With a cure, their lives would be totally different. As would hers, Samantha realized. With a cure…

When her gaze met Peter's, there was a hopefulness that was difficult to behold.

"If Sloan is alive, I don't want to put Melissa in danger again." Sebastian moved toward Melissa, assuming a protective stance close to her.

Peter held up his hand to quiet the young man. "We don't know for sure. Even if he is, he's turned his sights elsewhere."

"To me and my friends," Samantha interjected.

"Because it would have been too obvious if he'd come after you and the journals again," Diana said, motioning to the young doctor. "If it's Sloan, he's come after Samantha and Diego because one of your other friends gave you up. But who gave *them* up?"

It was Ryder who answered. "Ask around The Lair or any other similar club. Eventually, you'll end up at The Blood Bank. It's where all the curious and wannabes go in the hopes of finding the real thing."

"But it goes beyond that." Diana began to pace. "Someone pointed out Meghan to Sloan. Why?"

She snared Samantha's gaze. "Why?"

Samantha shrugged. "The rules are we keep our secrets to ourselves, but Meghan was a problem to some."

"To Foley?" Ryder asked.

"Foley? Who's Foley?" Sebastian asked.

"The vamp owner of The Blood Bank," Diana explained to her brother.

Samantha shook her head vehemently. "Foley wouldn't betray Meghan."

"How can you be so sure, Samantha?" Melissa asked.

"Because Foley is a businessman. All those missing vamps are costing him money," Peter answered. "That was clear from the night we paid him a visit."

Samantha considered Peter's words, and something else occurred to her. "Meghan and Blake both went missing from the private rooms, didn't they?"

"Yes," both Peter and Diana confirmed.

She looked from Peter to Diana and then to Ryder. "There are various vamps on duty there, night after night. But only one vampire who saw someone like Sloan with both of them. Only one who was on duty both times."

"Which means we need to pay another visit to The Blood Bank and our friend Foley. Maybe he can help us find out what's been going on with the vampire guarding those private rooms," Ryder said.

"Let's go." Diana walked toward the door when Melissa asked, "What if Simon… What do I do if he starts to weaken again."

Diana turned to Samantha. "How closely are a keeper and vampire tied? Would their physiologies react similarly?"

"Possibly," she replied.

Diana faced Melissa. "Take care of him the way you've taken care of Ryder."

In unison, both Melissa and Sebastian nodded.

Peter stepped beside Diana and shot an uneasy glance in Samantha's direction. "Do you think it's wise to take Samantha with us? They may still be after her."

It was Ryder who came forward to answer. "She's safer with us."

Samantha agreed. "Let's go then."

Chapter 29

Diego battled the waves of pain. He was chilled from the sweat pouring off him as his body slowly healed. Too slowly, he worried.

The one that Blake called "the professor" had taken great delight in trying out various things on him as well as draining a large amount of blood. Before Diego passed out, he'd overheard the professor telling his assistant that he needed the vampire blood for some experiments.

Diego wondered just what kind of experiments the sick old bastard did.

He heard the snick of the lock as it turned and raised his head. The assistant was leading Blake and Meghan back into the room. "The Doc says you're to feed your friend here. Keep him alive for more tests."

"Fuck you," Diego called out.

The professor's assistant only laughed and blasted Diego with the stun gun.

The energy sizzled along his body and Diego battled to hold onto the consciousness that was key if they were to execute Blake's plan.

The man laughed and left the room.

Immediately, Blake and Meghan came to Diego's side. They both wore worried looks, so Diego tried to reassure them with a weak smile. "I'll be fine. I just need a little…" He couldn't finish and was surprised he was that frail.

"Easy," Meghan said and laid a hand on his chest.

He tried to smile again, but his muscles didn't want to cooperate. In fact, he was finding it harder and harder to keep his eyes open. It occurred to him then that he might be too far gone to help his friends. "Blake," he said, but it was barely a whisper.

The vamp looked from Diego to Meghan, who suddenly seemed frightened. Blake tried to reassure her. "Don't worry, Megs. He promised."

"He'll drain me."

Diego shook his head. Or at least he thought he did. Everything in his line of sight was starting to darken. With the last of his power, he said, "Hurry."

Blake exposed Meghan's neck to him.

It was like tunnel vision. Suddenly all Diego could see was Meghan's strong pulse. He didn't know if he was moving toward her or she toward him, but abruptly that pulse was beneath his fangs.

He sank his teeth into her flesh and fed.

Her blood was hot and filled with the kind of power only vamp blood had, but not as powerful as older vamp blood. Meghan was still too young to carry the full strength that came with age.

He drank of her deeply and slowly became aware of his surroundings.

Blake was behind him, fiddling with the lock on the chains. The scratch and click of a successfully picked lock made him stop feeding.

Weakened, Meghan slipped to the ground.

Blake immediately raced to her side. "Megs?"

"I'm okay." Her voice was raspy. She gripped a hand to her neck, where blood still oozed from the puncture wounds.

The energy from her blood was already beginning to course through his veins, but it still wouldn't be enough if they were to complete their escape. He needed more. He needed Blake's blood.

As their gazes locked, Blake must have seen Diego's need. Meghan must have also, for she gripped Blake's arm to hold him back. "You didn't feed before. You're still weak."

Blake dropped a kiss on her lips. "I'll be fine, Megs. Don't worry about me."

Before Blake pressed himself close so that Diego could reach his neck, Diego noted the chill of the other vamp's skin. The slightly damp slickness that spoke of how weak Blake was.

Although Blake had always been a cocky, utterly royal pain in the ass, Diego had to admire the way the other vampire had behaved so far. His admiration made him hesitate as he brought his fangs close to the other vampire's neck. "Are you sure?"

"You remember your promise, Diego?"

"I'll take care of her for you, *amigo.*"

"Bollocks. Who knew it would end like this, mate." Blake pressed Diego's head forward, sinking Diego's fangs deep into his jugular.

* * *

Foley held his man by the neck, nearly a foot off the ground. The vampire kicked and grabbed, trying to break free, but Foley was too strong.

"Tell us, Mickey. Tell us how you betrayed Meghan and Blake." Foley repeatedly smashed the vampire against the rough brick wall until he was almost as limp as a rag doll.

"Let up, Foley," Samantha said.

Foley whipped his head around and nailed her with his gaze. "You'd let him go after what he did."

Ryder shook his head and laughed harshly at the other vampire's actions. "He can't tell us anything if he's not alive, Foley."

Chagrin flashed across Foley's face before he let Mickey slide down to touch the floor. He lessened his grip on Mickey's throat, but didn't let go. "Who paid you, Mickey?"

"An old guy. Said he wanted to meet someone who didn't want to be a vampire anymore. Like anyone would want that."

Mickey's voice had a thread of fear in it, and Samantha didn't doubt the reason why. Betraying another vampire carried a death sentence and Mickey knew it. It was probably the reason why he quickly tried to justify his actions to his boss.

"I knew you wanted her out of the way, Foley. She was a problem for you. I thought I was helping you. Helping her if this guy could do what he said."

"And Blake? Were you helping when you betrayed him as well?" Foley asked, clearly unmoved by Mickey's rationale.

Samantha watched Peter, Ryder and Diana as they stood quietly, observing. To a person, there was no pity or compassion for the traitor vampire. But despite what Mickey had done, Samantha couldn't justify the punishment Foley intended.

She stepped between Foley and the other vamp. "We need answers. We won't get them if you kill him."

"Who was the man who paid you, Mickey?" Foley asked.

"I don't know his name. All I have is a phone number." Even before Foley could pose the question, Mickey rooted through his pockets and pulled out a small piece of paper.

Foley passed the paper to Peter. "Cell phone number," Peter said out loud. "We can ask the phone company to try and give us a position."

"Then let's get moving," Ryder said. "Come on, Samantha."

Samantha met Foley's gaze and had no doubt what he planned. "Don't do this, Foley. He helped us."

"He helped himself, Samantha, and risked us all in the process. If you don't get this old psycho…" He didn't finish. He didn't have to. They all knew what would happen if they failed to find the person responsible for the kidnappings.

Behind her, Mickey had realized his fate. He opted for action instead of flight. Before she could do anything, he grabbed Samantha across the shoulders and brandished a knife to her throat.

"I'm leaving now, Foley. I'm—"

He didn't get to finish. Peter fired his gun.

There was barely a ripple in Mickey's body as the knife dropped from his grasp and he fell back.

She turned and stared into Mickey's wide-eyed gazed and the neat bullet hole smack in the middle of his forehead. "He can't be dead," she said. Bullets didn't normally kill vampires.

"Silver," Diana explained. "It's a special load. I gave Peter a clip in the car."

A special load? One reserved for when Diana had to deal with vampires?

Foley cursed beneath his breath. He nudged Mickey's body with the point of his boot. "Dead as can be."

"I'm not sorry, Foley," Peter said and holstered his gun.

Foley laughed out loud. "Seems to me you're getting to like this, dude. The darkness is a beautiful thing, isn't it?"

Peter didn't want to consider Foley's words. They struck a little too close to home. As much as he'd worried about the violence within Samantha, he knew he had much of the same violence within him. He'd unleashed it more than once to protect humans in his role as a law enforcement officer and it seemed he had no qualms about unleashing it to protect vampires as well. Maybe he and Samantha weren't all that different.

"He's not like us, Foley," Samantha said, slipping her hand into Peter's.

"Your heart is too soft, Samantha. You all are sorry pairs. I hope that now that you're done here—"

"We'll be going." Ryder nodded at Foley. "See you around."

"What about Mickey?" Diana motioned to the dead vamp's body.

Foley grinned. "Mickey's body will help remind everyone of our code."

With that, he tossed Mickey body across one shoulder and walked away down another corridor.

Peter asked, "Where's he going?"

"To a special room. One reserved solely for vamps," Samantha answered and moved toward the main club area.

Peter grabbed her arm. "What will he do in the—"

"He'll put him on display to remind everyone of our rules. To remind everyone of what we shouldn't do." A shiver tracked down her spine as she thought of Mickey's body, pinned on the wall like a butterfly on display. Until he became a big pile of dust. Like Esperanza soon would be despite how carefully they'd kept her body so Diego would have something to bury.

"Samantha?" Peter asked.

But she couldn't answer. Instead, she wrapped her arms around him, needing to feel his life. Needing the comfort that enveloped her when he returned her embrace.

Her friends might be dead. Dead like Mickey. Killed without hesitation by the man who was now holding her so gently.

She pulled away from him. How could they merge two worlds that were both filled with so much darkness? Would he one day terminate her existence if necessary? She was just a demon after all.

The comfort of his arms evaporated and when Peter stepped toward the door, she hung back, needing the space. Ryder strode past her and she found herself facing Diana. There was compassion on the woman's face and understanding. Samantha realized Diana comprehended Samantha's pain. She was someone Samantha could count as a friend. Diana nodded and slipped her arm through Samantha's. Together they walked out to the van where the two men waited for them.

Chapter 30

Peter flipped his cell phone closed with disgust.

"Phone company was willing to trace it, but couldn't. Seems someone disabled the GPS chip. The best they could do was provide the locations of the cell towers based on the last phone call."

He glanced down at his notes then turned to Diana. "Do you think Sebastian can get us an area to search based on the location of these towers?"

Peter sat on the bench seat by Samantha and took her hand while Diana called her brother. Samantha's hand was cold and damp. "Are you okay?"

"Just a little tired." As she faced him, he noted how pale she had become.

Ryder must have noticed as well since he said, "There's nourishment in the fridge in the back of the van."

Samantha shook her head vehemently. "No, I'm fine."

"Samantha, if you need—"

"No!" She pulled her hand from Peter's, and wrapped her arms around herself in a self-protective gesture.

Peter tried to embrace her, but she shied away from his touch. In the dim light from a streetlamp and the dome light Ryder had turned on for Diana, Peter tried to read Samantha's face for some hint of what she was thinking, but she had shut herself off from him.

It was a familiar look. He'd seen it the day she'd told him not to come by the shelter anymore. After last night, he hadn't expected to see that look any time soon, but obviously the events of tonight had taken a toll.

He could have pressed the issue, but decided against it. He suspected that would only push her further into her shell.

So he turned his attention to Diana, who was translating whatever information Sebastian had found onto a road map Ryder had dug out of the glove compartment. With her pen, she circled an area on the map.

The crackling sound of Sebastian's voice was audible but unintelligible. When she bid him goodbye, she repeated his report. "Simon awoke about an hour ago. He was agitated and afraid, but then he calmed. After about another hour, his vital signs strengthened."

"Which means?" Peter asked and looked to Ryder.

He shrugged and said, "You're barking up the wrong tree. There's obviously a lot I don't know about being a vampire."

Diana turned in her seat and laid a hand on Samantha's thigh. "Samantha," she said softly, as if recognizing that the other woman had withdrawn. "What do you think is happening with Simon?"

"The agitation…it could mean something bad is happening to Diego."

"And the calm?" Peter asked, wanting to comfort her, but restraining himself. He suspected it would only upset her right now.

"If Simon is calmer and improving, it could mean that Diego is regaining his strength. Maybe he's fed."

"Which means Diego may have escaped from Sloan," Ryder said.

"Or that Sloan is keeping him alive," Diana responded. "Maybe Sloan is still working on what he found in Frederick Danvers's last journal."

"Whatever it is, we're wasting time just sitting here. How far are we from where Sloan may be?" Peter motioned to the map in Diana's hand.

"At least an hour and the area Sebastian has pinpointed is still pretty big," Diana replied.

"Let's get moving then." Ryder started up the van and pulled away from the club.

"Maggie mentioned that Esperanza's body had been in a rural area near water." Diana motioned to one section on the map with a pen light. "There's a stream here that feeds this small lake," she added. Beside the stream Diana had noted, was a broken line indicating a proposed road. "If this map is old, there could be a road here."

"And buildings," Peter added. "But how will we—"

"I can feel him," Samantha said in low tones. "If Diego is still alive, I'll know he's around."

"Vamp radar?" Peter asked. "Do you all possess that or—"

"I've fed on him recently. It creates a bond for a little while," she admitted, her tone anguished.

Peter told himself not to be jealous. Samantha's life pre-Peter was none of his business. Not to mention that both Sofia and Samantha had said there was nothing going on there. Peter had been the only man in Samantha's bed.

That was what he told himself as he met Diana's compassionate gaze. Of all people, she would understand how difficult it was to be with a vampire. To deal with all the issues that entailed. Though Ryder appeared to be clueless about a lot of undead things. Maybe that made it easier for him and Diana.

But Samantha. Samantha was all vamp. Fully aware of the rules. Fully capable of feeding on both human and vampire.

So was he crazy to think that after all this was over, he and Samantha could continue their relationship? As Samantha met his gaze, he realized she was thinking the same thing.

Meghan cradled Blake's cold damp body. The signs of Diego's feeding were evident on Blake's pale skin. Two raw-looking puncture wounds that weren't healing because Blake was too weak. Because Blake was dying.

She could feel the lack of power in his body. The fading of his vitality as he continued to bleed.

She held him close and urged him to feed. "Please, Blake. Please," she pleaded, but he just weakly shook his head. When he spoke, his voice was so muted, she almost couldn't hear him.

"Let me go, love. You need…your strength."

Even speaking seemed to tax him.

She rocked him in her arms. Diego watched them intently, seemingly surprised by her concern for the punk vampire. "I thought the only emotion you had for him was hatred, little one."

Meghan stroked Blake's face and dropped a kiss on his forehead. "He kept me alive, Diego. He helped me."

"He sired you," he said with vehemence. "You wanted to kill him at one time."

"I did," she confessed, but raised Blake to her neck again, baring it for him. His head dropped away feebly when she released her hold. Tears of frustration stung her eyes.

She stroked his face again and he opened his eyes. They were a stunning shade of deep blue. She hadn't noticed before, but it was impossible to ignore them now as he swept his gaze over her face. He grinned then, surprising her. "You're…beautiful, love."

His body jerked against hers and that convulsion was followed by another and another.

Diego said, "He's in the last stages now. Soon there will be very little you can do."

"Please, Diego. I can't let him go," she cried out while trying to quiet Blake.

"Are you sure about this? It will weaken you," Diego replied.

"I'll take that risk."

Diego nodded and said, "He's your sire. That creates a special bond. Offer him your breast, but prepare yourself for what will follow."

When only a slight trembling remained in his body, Meghan held him to her breast. His eyes were open, but wide and slightly unfocused. His mouth slack and his breathing erratic. She cupped her breast and offered it up to him.

He refused her, but as she pressed him closer, his lips found the tip of her and suckled. His fangs elongated slowly. His eyes glowed with his transformation. But despite the glow, there was anguish there and once more, he tried to pull away. She would have none of it and with her greater strength, she forced his mouth close.

With an angry growl, Blake opened his mouth wide and bit down.

The pain was excruciating as was the pleasure that erupted between her legs. She was torn between pushing him away and pulling him closer and found herself giving in to the latter emotion. She grasped him tight as a searing hunger swept over her. The harsh suckling weakened her, but roused him.

Beside her naked thigh, he was growing hard and she needed it. Needed him. Somehow she straddled him and drove herself onto his erection, riding him as he fed from her. Driving them both to a climax that finally made Blake break free and roll her to her back so he could keep moving in her. Satisfying the sexual lust unleashed by his feeding.

Diego had warned her, but nothing could have prepared her for the sensations overwhelming her. For the languor sweeping across her body. For the need that made her clutch at Blake's shoulders and wrap her legs around his pumping hips.

"Magnificent," the old man said, shattering the moment.

Blake quickly moved away, blocking her body with his.

The old professor stood before them, a cattle prod in his hand. His assistant waited behind him. There was a leer on the younger man's face as he looked at her. She had no doubt that if left alone with her, he wouldn't hesitate to pleasure himself. But he would never get the chance.

Diego sprang into action.

The chain that had bound him to the beam looped around the man's neck and Diego pulled tight. The man's eyes bulged and he grabbed at the chain, trying to free himself as his face grew redder. The old professor grabbed the Taser from his assistant's hands and fired at Diego.

Diego's body jerked. As the professor increased the voltage, smoke curled from the spot in Diego's shoulder where the electrodes had struck.

Meghan stood there, Blake beside her, both of them paralyzed until Blake finally snapped to action and wrestled the Taser from the professor's hands. The old man jabbed the cattle prod into Blake's midsection, which sent him reeling backward.

Meghan grabbed Blake and kept him from falling, but she could tell the jolt had weakened him.

With Blake out of the way, the professor turned back to Diego, but it was too late to save his assistant. A last final jerk of the chain and the man's neck snapped. He dropped to the ground, dead.

The professor jabbed out with the cattle prod and caught Diego midchest. The jolt rocked Diego and dropped him to his knees, a surprised look on his face.

Blake struggled to his feet, intent on resuming his defense of the other vampire. He lurched forward again, grabbed the professor's arm, causing the prod to just graze Diego's body. Angry, the old man stunned Blake again. This time the blow dropped Blake to the ground.

He was about to jab Blake again, which would certainly have killed the vamp in his weakened state, when Diego grabbed the professor from behind and snared the cattle prod. But Diego didn't get a good grip on the old man, who backpedalled to the far side of the cell.

Meghan rushed to Blake's side as did Diego. Between the two of them, they got Blake on his feet. He was wobbly, but able to move with their help. "Let's go, Diego," Meghan said.

Diego shook his head. "No. We need to finish this today."

"Yes, we do," the old man said. From beneath his lab jacket, he pulled out a gun.

Diego laughed harshly. "Bullets can't stop me, old man."

The professor obviously thought they could. He fired twice, striking Diego low in his midsection.

Meghan watched as Diego stopped in his tracks. His body went still before he dropped to his knees.

He looked up, shock in his voice as blood poured from the

two bullet wounds. He was battling for consciousness as he uttered one word.

"Silver."

Chapter 31

They almost missed the turnoff for Lake Road. The highway exit was so new, it had only a temporary sign marking it.

For the first half mile or so, there was little except announcements for new luxury homes. Then, a few dirt roads leading away from the street both left and right. Based on the map, the lake was to the right and so they concentrated on those roads, looking for evidence that they had been recently used.

Samantha forced herself to concentrate, hoping to pick up some sign of Diego. If he was still alive, that was.

At the third turnoff, she finally sensed some power. "Slow down." She tried to focus, but it was still only a vague sense of another like her. At the next turnoff, it was stronger and by the next, even more discernible, but it dropped off shortly thereafter. "Turn back. It was the last road."

As they drove down the dirt path, Peter murmured, "Looks familiar, doesn't it."

At her questioning glance, he explained. "Last time, Sloan held Melissa in an old stable. The road leading to it was a lot like this."

"And so's the building up ahead," Diana added as they entered a clearing and encountered a one-story cement structure. There was nothing to identify it, but there were lights in the few windows along the front.

As Ryder stopped the van, the sound of gunshots shattered the night and Samantha experienced a huge surge of power. "It's Diego. He's been hurt, but…" The energy was too strong to belong to just one vampire. "Meghan and Blake. I think they're here as well. And alive."

"Let's go, then." Diana slipped out of the van, her gun drawn. Peter followed behind her, while Ryder and Samantha trailed along, defenseless except for their vampire powers.

The front door was unlocked. Diana raced down the hall, Peter at her back.

At the open doorway farthest from the entrance, they paused and then rushed in, guns drawn.

Samantha and Ryder stepped in behind them to find an almost unbelievable tableau.

Three vampires kneeled naked before an older man, who had a gun trained on them.

Samantha didn't think. She rushed to them. The old man said in warning, "Not another move or I kill all of you."

When she laid her hand on Diego's shoulder, the chill of his skin alarmed her. He was almost insubstantial.

At her touch, he whispered, "Silver. The bullets are silver."

She glanced down and noticed the blood covering the front of him. The silver was keeping him from healing. Worse, if it stayed inside him long enough, it would poison his system beyond repair.

"Drop the weapon, Sloan," Diana called out, inching slowly along the right side of the room.

Peter mirrored her actions, flanking the left side. Slowly, the two detectives shifted together until they formed a screen between Sloan and the vampires.

Sloan called out, "Stay out of my way."

"It's over. There's no sense in hurting anyone else," Peter said softly.

"You don't understand. They hold the key to life." Sloan waved the weapon. His tone was wild and Peter didn't know if they'd be able to reason with him.

"Is that what Frederick Danvers discovered? Is that what was in the journal you stole?" Diana asked.

A look of shock crossed the old man's features. "You know about the journal? About Melissa?"

"Remember me?" Ryder said and finally stepped forward where Sloan could not fail to recognize him.

Samantha realized the old man had lost what little control he'd possessed. He raised his gun, and she saw his intent. She couldn't let it happen.

Morphing, she raced in front of Ryder as Sloan and Diana fired.

Pain seared through her upper chest as the sound of gunfire erupted in the small room.

Ryder's arm came around her midsection as her legs buckled.

"Why?" Ryder asked as he kneeled beside her.

"Silver to the heart…fatal," she said and was surprised by how weak her own voice sounded. But she'd had no choice. The shot would have killed Ryder.

"Hold on, Samantha." Peter was there pressing his hand to her upper chest to staunch the blood.

"I have to get the bullet out," Ryder said. "There's a medical bag in the van. I'll be right back."

As Peter held Samantha, he watched Diana examine the body of Sloan for a pulse. Apparently there was none. Her bullets had done their work. Despite that, Diana turned over the old man and cuffed his hands, almost as if she didn't trust that he was really dead.

Peter didn't blame her. Sloan had already proven them wrong once before.

In the middle of the room, the one large vamp who'd been shot—Diego, Peter assumed—was now on the ground and the two younger vamps were hovering over him. They were trying to stop the bleeding much as he was. And much like he was, they seemed to be fighting a losing battle.

Peter looked down at Samantha, who had a small smile on her face. "It doesn't hurt," she said.

"What?" He applied greater pressure as yet more blood leaked from between his fingers.

"Dying. It doesn't hurt as much as I thought it would," she said in surprisingly calm tones.

He wanted to argue with her. He wanted to tell her she wouldn't die, but she was losing way too much blood. He didn't want to waste her last moments with a lie. "I love you."

She smiled, but it turned to a grimace of fear as she struggled for breath.

"Easy, love. Easy." He battled back the fear in his own voice to ease her discomfort.

Samantha cradled the side of his face. "I'm sorry we didn't have more time together."

Ryder returned and kneeled beside them. As he saw her condition, his look turned grim. "Whatever I do may not be enough."

"Hurry," Peter said, removing his hand from Samantha's wound so Ryder could reach it.

Diana stepped over to assist Ryder. She tore away the upper part of Samantha's shirt to expose the wound and dabbed the area with gauze to keep the area clean so Ryder could locate and extract the bullet.

Samantha moaned and shifted with Ryder's probing.

Peter held her tighter and murmured calm words to gentle her. It seemed to take hours for Ryder to pull out the silver bullet, although Peter knew it had only been minutes. Almost immediately, the flow of blood slowed, but she was still too pale and her breathing was shallow. Erratic.

Ryder moved away to help the other wounded vampire. "What can I do?" Peter asked Diana, fearing that what Ryder had done had not been enough.

"She may need to feed. Ryder has blood in the van."

With a nod, he took Samantha in his arms and followed Diana outside. She helped him get settled in the back of the van and removed a blood bag from a small refrigerator. "Do you need help?"

"I've never done this before."

She kneeled opposite him and brought the bag to Samantha's mouth. At the contact of the plastic with her lips, she roused. He saw confusion on her face, and then shame.

He realized she was hesitant to feed in front of him.

Cradling her cheek, he bent his head close to hers. "Please, Samantha. I don't want to lose you."

As he pulled away, her eyes began to glow and her fangs slowly inched down. He held the bag to her lips again and watched as she punctured the bag and fed.

He thought he would be repulsed, but instead, it was fascinating to see the change in her as she drank the blood. He could feel her body growing less limp and more substantial. Her skin warmed and gained color.

But not enough, he realized as she finished the bag and sagged back into his arms. The blood had only temporarily helped. Diana went back to the refrigerator, but there was no more.

"We'll have to get her back to town. There'll be blood at either the shelter or at Ryder's place."

Although Samantha's breathing was a little stronger, it was still too weak for his taste. "Can she make it back to town?"

"I don't know, Peter. Maybe Ryder can tell us once he's done inside," she said. "I'm going to go see if they need my help."

Peter nodded and leaned back against the side of the van, holding her tight, as if he could warm her with his body. Give her a little bit of his strength just with his nearness.

But with each minute that passed, her body became weaker and once again her breathing grew shallow and barely noticeable. He kissed her forehead. "Don't leave me."

He had barely uttered the words when the side door of the van slid open. Meghan and Blake sat on either side of Diego, holding him upright. A second later, Ryder tossed in the bodies of both Sloan and his assistant.

"Why are you bringing them?" Peter asked. Ryder looked his way and, seeing Samantha's condition, he picked up the dead assistant's body. "No way," Peter said.

Ryder snarled at him, "Squeamish? Well, they need to feed if they're to survive. Seems to me it's only fair."

"Ryder." Diana laid a hand on his arm. "Let the other three help themselves to these two. I'll take care of Samantha."

"No way, darlin'. I should be the one."

"Drive, Ryder. We'll need your strength to get all these people up to your apartment," Diana said.

As if recognizing the truth of her words, Ryder nodded, exited the van and closed the door behind him.

Diana moved over to where Peter held Samantha. As the three other vamps shared the corpses, Peter tried not to notice. Diana pulled closed a curtain to seal off the sight of what was happening.

Ryder started the van, jostling them.

Diana reached out to him. "She just needs a little to hold her over until we get back to the apartment. I can do that."

A confused whirl of emotions created a tumult within his brain. He wanted Samantha to live. He knew what it would take, but couldn't imagine anyone doing it. Much less his friend Diana.

But as she rolled up the sleeve of her black shirt to expose her forearm, he saw the scar there. The long-healed mark. In his mind, he pictured the two punctures in the middle of that wound before it healed as vampire bites did.

She pulled out a pocket knife.

"No." He stopped her when she would have cut her forearm.

It was almost as if stopping her had made the decision for him. He held out his free arm. "Cut me."

She knew him better than to question his instruction. Undoing the cuff on his dark blue shirt, she rolled it up to expose his skin. She raised the point of the knife to his wrist. "Ready?"

At his nod, she cut through his skin, just enough to bring blood to the surface.

"Now what?"

She motioned for him to bring his wrist to Samantha's mouth.

As soon as his bleeding arm touched Samantha's lips, she became alert. At first she only sucked with her mouth, but then her fangs slowly emerged.

Diana laid a hand on his shoulder. "The feeding…it may arouse other hungers."

Her meaning was clear. When he nodded, Diana left, closing the curtain tight to give them privacy.

When Samantha sank her fangs into his wrist, the pain jolted him from other musings. A mixture of revulsion and fascination swept over him as he observed her, and then something else awakened.

With each pull of her mouth came a tug at his groin, dragging passion to life even as he weakened.

"Samantha," he cried out as his erection became almost painful.

She pulled her mouth from his wrist and sat up, her color restored and her breathing stronger. She straddled him, returning to normal, her eyes losing their glow and her fangs retracting.

"Samantha," he pleaded again although he wasn't quite sure what he was begging for. But if he didn't get it soon, he'd die.

She knew. Her hands were warm as she stroked him. She kissed his lips and made love to him with her mouth, her tongue wet and deliciously wild as it danced with his. He clenched his hips and flexed upward into her hands, close to climax. So near to a release unlike any other he'd experienced before.

She took him into her mouth. Used her lips and tongue to drive him over the edge. His body was shaking. He was nearly close to losing consciousness when she reversed their positions and cradled him to her breasts.

"Peter, do you want me?" she asked even as she undid the buttons on her blouse.

Another jolt raced through him at the sight of her breasts and he immediately hardened again. He groaned and his head whirled with the untamed desire sweeping through his body.

Samantha asked again, "Do you want me, Peter?"

He answered her by taking the tip of her breast into his mouth and sucking on it.

She moaned and whispered, "It can be like this always, Peter. Always."

Oh please. He bit the tip of her as she stroked his erection. The thrall of vampire passion raced from her body to his. Desire so intense he knew it wasn't natural. It wasn't human.

"Is this what you want for us?" he asked even as he sucked at her breasts and, worked his way up to the edge of her lips, where the tiniest hint of fang was emerging. That didn't stop him. On the contrary, he traced the edge of her teeth with his tongue. When her fang nipped him, drawing blood, the coppery taste of it spiced his mouth.

Samantha's body was shaking and hot with the taste of his blood. Aching from feeding on his sexual release. It wasn't the woman holding him, even though she was fighting to retain her mortal form. It was the vampire, wanting him to give in. To beg him to be with her always.

It was why she couldn't answer him. She was afraid it would be the vampire answering. The vampire offering to make him like her so their love could be for always. So this passion would never end.

The van jolted over a bump, reminding her suddenly of where she was. Of why she was experiencing this sudden surge. Because he'd saved her life by feeding her. Because he loved her.

With a shudder, she forced away the unnatural hunger, and, like a balloon popping, the desire evaporated between them.

They were suddenly just sitting there, facing each other. Clothes torn and gaping open. Their breathing rough from the aftermath of the vampire desire.

Peter's eyes were wide, his pupils dilated with passion. "Is this what you want?"

It took all of her strength to take a deep breath, battle away the vampire and say, "I want you, but not like that. I want you to want the human in me."

It took a moment for her statement to register. Then he reached out and buttoned up her shirt. Reached down and put himself back in order.

Samantha wrapped her arms around herself, self-conscious, but he drew her close. She crawled into his lap and grabbed hold of his shirt. "It'll be all right." He brushed a kiss across her forehead.

But as she considered all that had happened, she wondered how anything could ever be right again.

Chapter 32

Somehow they got all of the injured vampires into Ryder's apartment.

While Melissa and Ryder tended to Meghan, Blake and Diego, Peter and Diana left to take care of the bodies of Sloan and his assistant.

Melissa took a quick look at Samantha's wound and given that it was almost totally healed, left her in a spare bedroom while she cared for the others. It was almost morning, so Samantha called the shelter to let everyone know she was fine. After, she let herself rest for a short time, needing to regain not only more of her physical strength, but some control over her emotions after what had happened with Peter.

A little over an hour had passed when she rose from the bed, borrowed a T-shirt from Melissa to replace her torn and blood-stained blouse, and checked on her friends.

She was surprised to find Meghan and Blake cuddled together in bed, holding each other as they slept. It was probably a combination of their weakness and the coming of the sun that kept them from rousing as she entered the room.

Diego, however, was alert as she sat on the edge of his bed. "How are you, *mi amigo?*"

He ran his hand over the wounds in his abdomen. "It's been a long time since I've been close to death. So close to welcoming the peace it would bring."

"I understand," she said and sighed harshly. "Except for losing Peter, death wasn't such a scary thing."

Diego was silent for a moment before he said, "Esperanza?"

"She's at your lair. We assumed you would want to say goodbye."

He gazed straight up at the ceiling, but that didn't stop her from seeing the tears that came to his eyes and spilled down the side of his face. "I should have protected her better."

"Sometimes we can't protect those we care about."

"Funny thing for you to say, *querida,*" Diego chastised.

She gave him a puzzled look.

"The shelter. All of us. Ryder. You've sacrificed yourself time and time again for so many," he explained.

Samantha shrugged, which brought a twinge of pain to her injury, reminding her of the truth of his words. "What else could I do, Diego?"

"Think of yourself first for once," he said. "The good detective. You love him. But I also suspect you're ready to sacrifice what you want so that he doesn't have to deal with the complications of loving a vampire."

They had been friends for too long, obviously. Diego had known exactly what she'd been thinking. She averted her gaze, afraid of what else he might see as she said, "Tonight in the van—"

"It was marvelous, Samantha."

Her head popped up at his comment. "You felt it?"

"We are all connected now. We all felt it, only…" His voice trailed off, his tone uncertain before he finished. "It was more than vampire, Samantha. It was what we all wished we still had, but can't because…"

"We're vampires. What we feel… It's all wrong, Diego. It's wrong to drag Peter further into my world."

Diego sat up in bed and gripped her hand tightly. "It was real, Samantha. It was more human than vampire. It can be what you've always wanted."

What she'd always wanted was to find real love and an honorable man to share it with. It occurred to her that she finally had just that. "A vampire and a human—"

"Do you see Ryder and Diana? Do you see how strongly they've bonded?"

"Foley says she is dark inside."

"Foley," Diego said with an annoyed and regal huffiness. "Foley's an idiot. She's dark, but it's the light of the love inside her that sustains him."

Samantha wanted to believe her friend. Wanted so much to think that it was possible for her and Peter to get past all that had happened in the past few days and give their relationship a real shot. "What if—"

"Regrets are for the weak, *mi amiga,* and you have never been weak. You proved that tonight," he said. Before she could say anything else, he dismissed her. "I am tired now. Go. Wait for the good detective to come back."

She did as he asked. Simon was comfortably settled on the sofa, reading a book. Melissa was on the phone, giving someone instructions and indicating that she'd be at the hospital later.

A hard life that of a keeper, Samantha thought, realizing

that the young pregnant woman had just spent the better part of the night tending to her friends and now had to deal with her everyday life. But then Sebastian stepped out of the kitchen and came to stand beside his wife.

Sebastian held her and whispered, "I'll walk you over. Stay to make sure you're fine."

They shared a kiss before they left the apartment. The emotions the scene roused were too strong. Reminded Samantha too painfully of how she wanted someone to share her life.

She had to leave. Go back to the shelter and try to get her life back in order. But the front door opened before she could reach it.

Diana and Peter walked in. Peter stopped short before her and shoved his hands in his pockets. He jingled the change there in a nervous habit that was becoming increasingly familiar and endearing.

"How are you?" he asked.

"Feeling better. And you?"

He shot an anxious glance over his shoulder and Diana took the cue. She walked to the back of the apartment and the stairs that led to another floor.

"I'm…confused. Concerned. We just checked two bodies into the morgue and had to explain why we had them." He stared at his feet and shook his head. "I don't think they'll charge us. After all, Sloan was wanted for five counts of murder and kidnapping, but we did mess up the crime scene. They may ask for my badge. And Diana's."

"I'm sorry. I never—"

He raised his hand abruptly to silence her. "Don't apologize. And don't run away, because right now, you're the only thing in my life I'm sure about."

"Me?" she nearly croaked. "You're sure about me?"

"Yes. You," he answered, no hesitation or doubt in his voice. He took a step closer. "Whatever else may happen—"

"Whatever else? Like what? Maybe getting you killed?" She backed away from him.

"That won't happen. We took care of Sloan." He walked toward her and kept on walking until he had her backed against the wall where she could no longer run.

"If it's not Sloan, it'll be someone else. Something else," she said.

"We can handle it together, Samantha. You don't have to be alone anymore." He cradled her head in his hands and gently urged her face up so that she couldn't avoid him. "I don't want to be alone anymore."

"I can't give you anything you want. No kids—"

"Last time I looked, there were a few at the shelter."

"What about what happened last night?" she countered, hoping it had been as scary for him as it had been for her. She'd been at the point of turning him and if it hadn't been for his strength in questioning her, she would have.

"You stopped."

"This time."

He leaned his forehead against hers and said, "You're trying to make this harder than it has to be."

He didn't give her a chance to respond, stealing away any protest with his kiss.

"Peter, you don't know what you're saying," she argued when she was able to draw a breath.

"But I do," he whispered against her lips. "And if you're willing to try, I promise there won't be a day that goes by that you won't feel this way."

Samantha could battle a lot of things, but not a promise like

that. There was no denying the way he made her feel. Happy.
Hopeful. Human. Alive.

After over a century without such emotions, she was willing to accept his promise and, in exchange, give him one of
her own. "I swear that there won't be a day that goes by without my loving you. Without holding you to your promise."

He smiled and pressed his body against hers. "Will you
hold me to it soon?"

"Is now too soon?"

He picked her up in his arms, and she pointed him in the
direction of the spare bedroom.

It was never too soon to get started with the rest of your life.

* * * * *

Dear Reader,

When I create a story, my goals are twofold. First, to develop characters who come alive. Second, to draw attention to an issue that I think is important. The issues have ranged from discrimination (Now and Always, September 1999) to battling self-esteem problems (Danger Calls, June 2005). In Temptation Calls, the issue was violence against women. I wanted to show how a woman can not only survive such violence, but be strong and caring enough to reach out to others who are suffering a similar plight. In a fictional world peopled with vampires, Samantha Turner accomplishes just that, but there are many women in the real world who are still suffering.

If you are a victim of domestic violence or suspect that a friend or family member is a victim, you can help stop the cycle by breaking the silence. Help is available at the National Domestic Violence Hotline at 1-800-799-SAFE. If you are a victim of rape or a sexual assault, or suspect that a friend or family member is a victim, help is available at the National Sexual Assault Hotline at 1-800-656-HOPE.

Thank you.
Caridad Piñeiro Scordato

Coming in November from

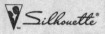 Silhouette®

INTIMATE MOMENTS™

and author

Brenda Harlen
Dangerous Passions
IM #1394

With a hit man coming after her,
beautiful Shannon Vaughn was forced to
go on the run with Michael Courtland,
the sexy P.I. assigned to protect her. But
as the enemy closed in, Shannon realized
she was in greater danger
of losing her heart....

*Don't miss this exciting story...
only from Silhouette Books.*

Available at your favorite retail outlet.

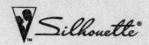

SIMCNM1005